Heads Ripe for Plucking

Heads Ripe for Plucking

Mahmoud Al-Wardani

Translated by
Hala Halim

The American University in Cairo Press
Cairo • New York

First published in 2008 by
The American University in Cairo Press
113 Sharia Kasr el Aini, Cairo, Egypt
420 Fifth Avenue, New York, NY 10018
www.aucpress.com

Dar el Kutub No. 4341/08
ISBN 978 977 416 188 9

Dar el Kutub Cataloging-in-Publication Data

Al-Wardani, Mahmoud

      Heads Ripe for Plucking / Mahmoud Al-Wardani; translated
by Hala Halim.—Cairo: The American University in Cairo Press, 2008
      p.   cm.
      ISBN 977 416 188 2
      1. Arabic fiction   I. Halim, Hala (tr.) II. Title
      813

1 2 3 4 5 6 7 8   14 13 12 11 10 09 08

Designed by Sally Boylan
Printed in Egypt

Acknowledgments

While avowing full responsibility for the text, I wish to point out that the passages presented as quotations from Iqbal Bakri's *Saratan al-rawh* (Cancer of the Soul) are extracted from a book by my late friend Arwa Salih that bears the same title. For the events of al-Husayn's martyrdom narrated here I consulted a substantial number of medieval chronicles.

Due acknowledgment should be given to the works of the late intellectual Hadi al-Alawi and to Muhammad Husayn al-Aaraji's book *Jihaz al-mukhabarat fi-l-hadara al-islamiya* (The Intelligence Apparatus in the Islamic Civilization). Finally, I had recourse to most of the testimonies and autobiographies of detained Communists, as well as Dr. Rifaat al-Said's book *Al-Jarima* (The Crime).

Part One

OH WELL, IT'S TIME I GOT SOME REST after all. I caught the last train—or so I was told—at the last minute, just as it was starting to drag its carriages slowly out of the station, the screeching of its wheels mingling with the sound of the diesel engine. As I came from afar I had my eyes glued on the train, which was brand new, its trunk sparkling in the dusk, as if it had just come fresh from the factory.

I raced down the slope that overlooks the station with an impetus I couldn't curb, and with amazing agility got onto the last carriage and made straight for the roof of the train. My companions who'd preceded me were sitting around in groups, eating, smoking, and chatting, everyone enjoying the refreshing breeze wafting from the fields. I found myself telling them my story. I said I'd caught the last train, that they themselves might have seen me and known that I'd relied on myself alone. Then I threw in that I deserved to get some rest, after all, and that this might well be my last trip.

1

I sat there overjoyed, wondering just how to celebrate. I got up and broke into a sprightly dance, bounding down the roof of the train, with my eyes shut for a few seconds and my arms outstretched to bask in the mild daylight, the sky above open and clear. Then I'd shut my eyes again and reopen them before leaping across the gap between one carriage and another. But one time, when I opened my eyes, I did not manage to duck at the right moment, so the first iron bridge hacked off my head. At first, I sensed my body separating from me, and how it pained me that it kept staggering on its own with no control over its steps until I fell under the wheels, while my head was impaled atop the iron bridge with my eyes open, gazing toward the south.

I remain until this minute open-eyed, suspended between the pinnacle of joy and the shock of the iron bridge, gazing at the sky until the sun sets when I rest for a little while and brace myself for a sun that shows no mercy all day long.

1

This was not the first time I parted with my head; I had parted with it several times before, just as others who preceded me had likewise parted with their heads.

And was the first among them the "Master of Heaven's Youth," notwithstanding that his noble head was oftentimes graced with the munificent hand of his grandfather, which he often caressed? Regardless, al-Husayn's head lay one evening in front of Ubaydallah ibn Ziyad, the agent of the new caliph, who was hard at it day and night exacting the oath of allegiance in all the cities on pain of death. Just then, Ubaydallah was poking the noble mouth and jabbing the tip of his sword between its teeth, before it was to be carried with the remains of al-Husayn's people and his enslaved women to the residence of the new caliph.

Indeed, the noble head escaped later, while it was being conveyed with the procession of captives on the way to Damascus, the seat of the Ummayad court, and landed in the arms of a woman known as Umm al-Ghulam in one of Cairo's alleys, an incident the veracity of which some have doubted on the grounds that Cairo had not yet been built at the time.

Barely fifty years had passed since the death of the Prophet when the head of his daughter Fatima's son was severed and his descendants were mutilated in this shameful fashion. Al-Husayn's may have been among the first heads that valiantly went forward to meet their ordained fate. He paid no attention to the advice given him by Abdullah ibn Mutie when he resolved to leave Mecca for Medina, fleeing from al-Walid ibn Utba ibn Abi Sufyan, who sought to secure the oath of allegiance for the new caliph Yazid in the wake of the death of the latter's father, Muawiya, who had fought al-Husayn's father, Ali ibn Abi Talib. When he learned of al-Husayn's intention, Abdallah ibn Mutie advised him not to head for Kufa, that ill-omened city that had witnessed his father's murder. "Be on guard," he reiterated. "The people of Hijaz revere no one more than you. Therefore summon your followers to you there."

It thus became clear to al-Husayn that Yazid had every intention of usurping the oath of allegiance or killing him just as Muawiya had brought about his father Ali's downfall and usurped the caliphate. Was history to repeat itself until the progeny of the Prophet would be plucked by the root and decimated? And yet, al-Husayn continued on his way in the company of his sisters Umm Kulthum and Zaynab, his nephews, and his brothers Abu Bakr, Jaafar, and al-Abbas, leaving behind only his brother Muhammad ibn al-Hanafiya.

It was only a few days after he had settled that one of the notables of Kufa went to him. He brought al-Husayn fifty messages from the nobles and chiefs asking him to come to them that they might pledge their allegiance to him so he would lead the insurgency against the corrupt caliph whose father had imposed him on the Muslims by sheer force. Messengers soon flocked to him with letters that filled two saddlebags urging him to set out from Iraq and continue on until he had vanquished and overthrown the caliph. Al-Husayn's response was an identical letter in which he informed everyone that he was sending them his paternal cousin, Muslim ibn Aqil, who was among the most trustworthy of his people, to get to the heart of the matter and let him know what he had ascertained. For al-Husayn was adamant not to repeat his father's tragedy, which he could not for a minute forget, and resolved to take every precaution.

At Kufa, Muslim hid in the house of al-Musayyab where the followers of al-Husayn came to him in secret. Word of his whereabouts spread and naturally reached the prince of Kufa, al-Nuaman ibn Bashir, as well as the heads of the new caliph Yazid's intelligence apparatus, Muslim ibn Said al-Hadrami and Umara ibn Uqba, who were both charged directly by him to keep a close watch on al-Husayn's followers. Without a moment's hesitation, they both immediately apprised him of what was going on in this remote spot, out of reach of his direct control. Responding in writing, Yazid ordered al-Nuaman removed and replaced by Ubaydallah ibn Ziyad, emphasizing to the latter in the letter of appointment that his mission was first and foremost to arrest Muslim ibn Aqil without fail and by any means.

Before the first night after Ubaydallah ibn Ziyad's appointment had elapsed, Muslim had fled in disguise to the house of Hani ibn al-Urwa, one of the notables of Kufa, to prepare for a more advanced stage of planning for the insurgency. He obtained pacts and oaths of allegiance to al-Husayn from all the followers who sought him out there, until they numbered eighteen thousand men.

As for the new prince, Ubaydallah, he had all but run out of strategies when he thought of turning to a client of his from the Levant, a man called Aqil whom he charged with the search for Muslim, starting out from the Great Mosque, where he was likely to find the beginning of the trail that would lead to the center of the rebellion. Just before Aqil left the prince's mansion, Ubaydallah gave him a sack containing three thousand dirhams. Indeed, Aqil succeeded in his mission to infiltrate al-Husayn's followers and hence found out the whereabouts of al-Husayn's emissary, Muslim.

At first, he resorted to a ruse in order to secure Muslim's head. He summoned Hani ibn al-Urwa, who was sheltering the fugitive, to the emirate palace. When Hani was brought in by the soldiers he, of course, refused to deliver his guest. Thus began the first season of beheadings, which would only continue to escalate.

2

EVERY MORNING, THE SUN SMACKS ME across the face and I open my eyes wearily into an onslaught of rays: thus begins a new day. On summer mornings like this, swarms of flies gnaw at me. I while away the time awaiting the afternoon breeze that will give me some respite from the bites by recalling earlier beheadings I underwent.

I couldn't believe I'd made it as I settled into my seat on the airplane getting ready for take-off and, fastening my seatbelt, closed my eyes.

Here I am after ten years broken up only by three vacations, each one a month long, which passed in the wink of an eye. Before I knew it, I'd find myself back in a hellhole that, in hindsight, I've no idea how I managed to bear. I'll make up for all those years with Nagat, Heba, and Ali in the Alexandria apartment I bought and even got to furnish on my last vacation. It's time I got some rest, some sense of calm. I have a month ahead of me, and then I'll get going on my project. I've now amassed all of $100,000 in the three trust funds in the bank. And that's apart from my private account that keeps me from dipping into the trusts, plus the taxi, which nets a minimum of three hundred pounds a month.

As for Nagat—she of the cutest belly and the most scrumptious navel among all the women I've known—I'm going to nibble at every inch of her. She'll lie beneath me and writhe the minute I bring out my surprise gift for her from the carry-on bag: a *collier* and a matching bracelet that set me back two thousand dollars.

As the airplane started to take off, the lights flickered and were turned off, then the sound of the engine drowned out everything else.

I was thinking that the last three years had been different from all the ones before them over there. When I moved ten years ago to 'the Mermaid,' as they like to call this town in the Gulf, having landed a contract with a school, I sent in my resignation from the post of librarian in the headquarters of the ministry, just to make sure I'd burned my bridges. Mine was an uncommon specialization—proof of which was that the number of students in the Archives and Librarianship Department at the university never exceeded two hundred in any year's class. So for me to end up working as a librarian who sits around doing nothing all day long and can't even make ends meet meant that grabbing the chance of a lifetime was a foregone conclusion. Within two months, I'd also gotten an evening job as an accountant for al-'Isa'i Trade Company, and my old passion for fixing electric appliances also opened doors. Soon, I was going to the houses of colleagues and acquaintances to fix their appliances and satellite dishes, both services for free, and, having gained access to people's houses, I started giving private lessons in homes from sunset until ten in the evening. When I went home at the end of the day I'd be dead tired, overcome with sleep the minute I opened the door of the room I shared with four Egyptians, a Palestinian, and a Sudanese. I barely remembered Nagat and the children, except at the beginning of the month when I sent them their allowance.

I worked seven days a week. I'd asked Abu Khalid to give me access to the office after the Friday prayers so that I could catch up on the backlog of work I claimed was piling up—and I didn't request overtime. This was one of my first tactics to gain their confidence, and it worked: they transferred me to the headquarters in the capital. There, things began to look up, and my savings just multiplied, and this, in turn, motivated me to double the accounting I did on the side for the small-time traders who cropped up all the time, now that I knew all the ins and outs. There was so much going on: agencies, stores, supermarkets, and shopping malls that sprung up overnight into which they'd stuff tons of merchandise brought in from the four corners of the earth. It was as if all the locals worked as traders—but then, who were the buyers? No matter, all I cared about was that each of these merchants occasionally needed some small job done for him, and I was the man who delivered in a single evening.

The first five years were the toughest. I had to buy the apartment in Faysal Street at the beginning of the Pyramids district, then there was the apartment in the Mustafa Pasha Towers in Alexandria, and the taxi. Actually, the taxi was an investment: I arranged with Muhammad Saad, the driver, to settle the accounts with Nagat every week. And I taught her how to go over the accounts carefully with him by checking the meter. So the Lada covered the children's expenses and I devoted myself to saving.

Nagat would be there to receive me at the airport, with Heba and Ali. I called her up last night and asked her to leave the stuffed pigeons and the rolled vine leaves—stuffed as well—in the oven so they'd keep warm, and come to the airport at 11 a.m.

In just three hours you'll be in my arms, Nagat. I'll buy a bottle of Chivas Regal from the duty free store and pour it out on her bellybutton then sip all night. I have $100,000, with which I'll open a mall in the Pyramids district that'll be the talk of the town. I'll call it the Hidaya Right Guidance Mall and it'll make me the owner of the fourth mall in all of Egypt. It'll be two stories high at first, then I'll add a third. The plot of land I bought for it is as big as the plans I worked out over years on end. I managed to secure it during my first year abroad with a down payment to my colleague the mathematics teacher who was looking for a buyer.

I wasted no time on the flight, and kept asking the hostess for coffee after coffee so that I'd stay alert and ready for the long day that lay ahead of me. First, I'd have to give my documents to Dirbala, the customs clearance man. I had everything worked out: I called him up and let him know my arrival time so that he'd take care of everything while I went home with Nagat and the children. He'd done the customs clearances for all the appliances I'd brought back on previous trips.

For three years, Nagat, I settled for phoning you once every month or two. Then, of course, it'd slip my mind amid all the work that had to be done—they sometimes sprang business trips on me to one of the towns close to the Gulf, or to the hinterland towns in the middle of the desert to get something or other done for one of the branches of the company. Deep down, I was satisfied that the children were getting their allowance, and felt there was no need to rush things as I edged, slowly but surely, toward the figure I had set for my savings. I replaced women with porno videos after three experiences that each left me more terrified than the one before it. Every time, I thought I'd repent, and would even make a vow to myself, but circumstances would bring me face to face with irresistible temptations. So I went for videos of which there were an endless variety, some pairing men with women, others men with men, and yet others women with women, and in fact there were even films starring famous Arab actresses and dancers.

I felt totally safe picking any of the women performing on the screen in front of me and fantasizing about her at my leisure. There was no need for risky adventures, like that time one of my colleagues took me along to a "house" of Filipinas. We were in the Mermaid where legends about the tightness and smallness of Filipinas' vaginas echoed like drumbeats. I went to bed with one of them, but it was only minutes before she started screaming when she saw my organ. I put on my clothes and left; then, when I'd reached the top of the street, I thought of going back since I'd barely gotten to know the woman. I turned to find that the police had surrounded the area: my friend and I ran as fast as our feet would carry us, with me nearly pissing my pants.

The second time was with Abla, whom I shall never forget. She was the daughter of Zayd, my Yemeni colleague in al-'Isa'i Company. After I'd fixed all Zayd's electric appliances without asking for a penny, he agreed to negotiate for me with the land-lord—my being a single man made me unwelcome among families—so that I could rent the small apartment adjacent to his in the residential building that was quite close to the offices of the branch of the company. I actually didn't notice Abla at first; after all, she was just a fourteen-year-old girl. If I remember cor-rectly, she was the one who made a pass at me. Whenever we met on the street, she'd stop me and practice on me, mimicking the way Egyptian actresses speak in movies and TV dramas while I coached her with the accent. She ended up sneaking into my apartment. At my hands, she learned the arts of heavy petting and the sexual positions we explored together in my bed. The challenge lay in the imperative of keeping her virginity intact, which I vowed to take the utmost care with. But then we were almost caught in the act when her mother barged in one day. With the doorbell ringing insistently, I got dressed and left Abla in the one bedroom in the house and pulled the door shut behind me. The woman started working on me the minute I opened the door. Knowing that her husband was out of town, she hung around in the living room, which was the first she'd seen of it since I moved in. She asked about her husband and I said he was away on a trip. She gave a little smile and said she knew that. I went on about how risky it was if someone dropped by and found us together. She stormed out angrily. Abla, who'd been waiting in the other room stark naked, unable even to put on her clothes, had a fit of uncontrollable sobbing. For months afterward I suffered from impotence and requested to be transferred to another branch of the company and finally got my wish.

The third time was with a local girl. She contacted me and we talked on the phone for a month until she trusted me. We spent the following month having phone sex several times a day. By the third month, I was ready to risk my life to meet her. I almost jeopardized everything as I roamed the streets, gazing up at the houses and eavesdropping by windows and at intersections. Suddenly, she called me and threatened that unless I gave up trying to find her, she'd cease to phone me altogether. My obsession spun out of control now that I knew she recognized me and was watching me rove through the city stalking the slightest trace of her. Then she was as good as her word and cut me off remorselessly. Our story ended after three months, without my ever having gotten her phone number.

So videos substituted for women; and then there was the homemade date liquor, the arak that goes straight to your head after the third glass. I somehow managed to get through month upon month and year upon year with the goal I had set for myself coming ever closer. But now that I've accomplished my goal, I am suddenly startled by a heaviness that bears down on my chest from time to time. The work that lies ahead—opening two or three branches of the mall—is as much as the work of the previous ten years put together. Only when I've got it finished can I really rest. I'll bide my time until Ali is through with school and the four years of undergraduate studies, and is ready to take over from me. By then Heba will be someone's spoiled and pampered wife and I'll still be sending her monthly allowance without fail. Nagat will be pushing forty and we'll have a few years together ahead of us that will surely be the most wonderful of our lives.

3

I WAS SLAIN TOO when I was a boy . . .

By 10 a.m. the bus taking us on the trip hadn't moved. The chaperones were sitting up in front after they'd checked on us one by one, again and again, then had us get off the bus to do a headcount all over again. We were all first-year pupils, but from different classes. I'd turned fifteen that day, January 18, 1977, and was planning to celebrate my birthday with my classmates as soon as we reached Port Said. Once we got there, the chaperones would let us loose on the town until the evening, as they always did on trips, and go off on their own, after arranging with us to meet at the bus at the end of the day.

The headmaster arrived finally and when we heard the engine start we went wild. When we'd reached Manial Street, we started cheering the driver on:

"Clever driver:

Take us to Qanater!"

Nagi, whom we all knew because he'd had to repeat the grade since he was often absent and played hooky, cheered, "Long live Mr. Azmi! Long live Mr. Rakha! Long live Mr. Abd al-Wahid!"

He didn't cheer for the fourth chaperone, Tawfiq Aydarus, whom we all hated and even wished to see dead because of his cane—he used it to give a beating to anyone who crossed his path during break time.

We finally reached the end of Manial Street, and when the bus swung in the direction of the Muhammad Ali Palace, it suddenly ground to a halt. But we just went on singing at the top of our voices. I was happy I had thirteen pounds that my mother had somehow managed to cobble together for me. Until last night, my dad was dead set against giving me more than the five pounds he'd decided on. My mom, though, slipped me an extra eight pounds, saying that I should buy whatever I needed, and not to worry about bringing any money back with me. Still, if I could buy two kilos of American apples and a tube of Signal II toothpaste, she'd be pleased, but if I couldn't that was fine too— the important thing was that I should take care of myself. I made my calculations carefully: a checkered BVD shirt, a pair of jeans (Lee, Wrangler, or FUS), and a pack of Marlboros that I'd smoke there to celebrate my birthday. But I had to keep enough on me to buy mints or chewing gum before I went home because my mom couldn't help crying when she smelled cigarettes on me, but she never told my father who though nothing of beating me even though I was a grownup now.

The bus was parked a long time. I craned to see past the classmate sitting beside me and found the street teeming with angry-looking people. They were pouring in from the side streets, gathering and crossing the Nile shouting. When the bus started up amid the loud honking of cars, one of the chaperones barked instructions that we all stay put in our seats. The crowds outside were thickening and though I couldn't catch what people were chanting it was clear they wanted to band together. They were the ages of my father, uncles, and cousins. The bus swerved and I recognized al-Sadd Street in Sayyida Zaynab district. I saw women in galabiyas and black wraparounds, some barefoot with children clutching at their hems, rushing out of the intersecting alleyways ahead of us. Then the bus came to a standstill and the bald driver turned to us and slapped his palms together.

A long time passed. Some of the pupils were smoking in the back of the bus, having taken their cue from the chaperones. In fact, three of the chaperones had slipped out, one after the other, leaving only one teacher on board. After a while, we shoved that chaperone out as well and one of us forced the door open and we all followed him out shouting. We melted into the huge crowd around us. All I had with me was my bag, which was empty except for the sandwiches my mother had given me. Nagi and Umar, the only two pupils from my class on the trip, joined me as I cut through the crowd. Everyone around us was shouting agitatedly and I couldn't figure out what it was all about. When we'd made it to the top of Port Said Street we found pupils from the Khedival Secondary School, Sabil Umm Abbas School, and the Hilmiya Commerce School gathered. They were chanting after someone:

"Gihan, is it true
that Ford fucked you?"

I found it really funny and was chuckling as I watched them, but they looked pretty serious. The world seemed vast just then and the three of us felt we could do just as we pleased. We looked at each other and burst out laughing and clapping. Then we cheered along with the others:

"Gihan, is it true
that Ford fucked you?"

The crowd was growing by the minute and the public buses and trams had stopped. "Looks like we won't be going on that trip," Umar said, leaning over and raising his voice above the din. Nagi and I answered in unison, "We're on the trip!"

We laughed again and, still close together, surged forward with everyone around us toward the square. There we found people holding up a boy wearing eyeglasses who was chanting:

"He dresses like a bridegroom

while we sleep ten to a room."

I was sure the boy meant Anwar Sadat: he was the best-dressed man I'd ever seen, and slim and always happy, his ready smile showing off his white teeth. The people knew just who was meant but they weren't afraid of Sadat; if anything, it just made them chant louder. The crowds were lining up in front of the Sayyida Zaynab police station, their cheering growing frenzied as they repeated after another man they held up who was waving his fists:

"They had us down to tattered clothes

and now they take our bread loaves."

What they were saying hit the mark and they were not afraid of anyone, not even of Sadat or State Security, so I chanted along. As for the Sayyida Zaynab Police Station, its notoriety had reached us all the way in Manial. Woe be to anyone who even came near it! Our classmates had told us stories about people they knew who'd been whipped and beaten, sometimes even killed, in that place. I tried to get a glimpse of its façade and made out some people carrying huge pipes or maybe logs of wood and shoving them forcefully against the outer gate of the police station. The chanting grew louder as everyone egged them on to break the gate:

"Give us democracy,
our life's a misery."

Suddenly, bullets flew from somewhere, hitting in the first round the ones who were trying to break down the gate. I caught sight of their silhouettes dropping at a distance while others turned round to flee. A stampede in the opposite direction had begun. It was essential that Nagi, Umar, and I stick together, what with the pressure on all sides and the risk of tripping and falling to the ground any minute. Nagi shouted in his croaky voice, "Hold on to each other! Careful now."

I was scared and felt hungry when another round of shooting started. I knew the relatives of two people who'd died in custody in the Sayyida Zaynab Police Station. The superintendent of that police station would park a van with its back to the Sharq Cinema in Sayyida Zaynab Square during the matinée. Then he'd pack the van with pupils playing hooky and keep them in custody for two or three days. I let myself be carried along with the rushing crowd, while making sure I kept my grip on Umar's hand. But my eyes watered as the pungent smell intensified and rose in my throat. I tried to run and pulled Umar to get away from it. It was clear, in any case, that I had to forget about the trip. Right beside me I saw a man running and holding up his arm splattered with blood, which made me grip Umar harder and practically drag him along. The chanting had died down, giving way to screams and curses on the government and the president. When my feet stumbled on the tram rails I realized we'd managed to get away from the battlefield and the gunshots, the reports of which still echoed.

4

IN THE MORNING THE SUN GIVES ME no respite. In summer it gets going very early, waking up the flies that worry at me until the night falls, so that by midday my skin will have cracked. It is then that the pain is at its most excruciating and I begin to slowly recollect what my head underwent at one time or another.

When they built the hospital on the outskirts of our small town by the river it made life a bit easier: only two years ago we had to travel to the capital. For me, the whole six days that the surgery lasted were sheer torture. What bothered me, though, was not so much the surgery as the two days it took to get there and back again. It was the business of boarding the train with all the terror that came with it, the sound of the rails crashing, and my having to depart from the normal flow of my day, which I control and do with as I please.

So he said to himself as he quietly and meticulously packed his underwear, nightshirt, and slippers into his small suitcase.

He had only a few hours to go before hailing a cab that would get him to the hospital in less than an hour. He smiled when he realized he had almost called his wife to hand him his tooth-brush and shaving set, which was the routine whenever he was about to go on a business trip to a nearby town. He considered snatching a catnap to pass the few minutes in which he was supposed to say goodbye to his wife and two daughters. Like the rest of the inhabitants of the city above the age of eighteen, he had to check in once every two years to get any damage in his head fixed. The doctors would hack off the head at the throat and send it to the maintenance department, where pro-grams were downloaded and spare parts installed in place of damaged segments. During this procedure, which usually took four days, one stayed at the hospital without a head, unable to get to the bathroom without the help of the female nurses. It actually caused him more anguish than the surgery itself that, for over twenty-five years now, to use the toilet he needed the help of a woman nurse who saw nothing of him but his urine and feces.

He would spend the rest of the day lying down and chatting with his ward companions in the beds closest to him. Of course their conversation tended to be disjointed and somewhat comi-cal, since each of them was at a different stage of the procedure and a voice that issues only from the lower half of the larynx hisses out before it can be shaped by the tongue muscles and lips. On winter days like these, he said to himself, we'd chase the sun around through the wide terraces and passages in the wards. Bumping into each other, we'd exchange words of apol-ogy and introductions, and many of us would even arrange to meet after we were discharged. Then and there, of course, one gives any name. In the euphoria of being discharged, some of us would stop by reception on our way out to ask for the names of others who had been in the same ward. But once out of the hospital, none of us has the time and we soon forget all about it.

He stretched out on his bed in the grip of a migraine attack. For two years now, his head had gone without maintenance, and it was time he was relieved of the buzz in his ears, the constant din that sometimes prevented him from getting any work done. Although he was hungry, the mere thought of the smell of food made him nauseous. His wife would be going to fetch the girls from their school in a little while. He would then say goodbye to them, pick up his suitcase, and go to the hospital.

Where part of the sky was visible through the window he saw clouds gathering. He felt cold, but was too lazy to pull the blanket over his body and just lay huddled there. The phone rang. It was a woman colleague calling to say goodbye and relay the greetings and good wishes of the rest of his colleagues and subordinates. He thanked her and asked her to let everyone know how touched he was by this gesture, then had to hastily end the conversation as the doorbell rang. It was not the time his wife usually came home, and in any case she would use her key to get in. Through the peephole he saw a boy holding a basket of flowers. He thrust a banknote toward him with a word of thanks. When he put the basket on the table he saw the card scribbled over with the names of his colleagues and subordinates. He was smiling as he walked back to his bedroom. There was hardly anyone he could think of who bore him a grudge or with whom he'd had any problems. In fact, he barely knew any of them. And yet, he was always courteous and friendly with everyone, as well as cautious, indeed stingy. It was not just the handful of pounds he got at the beginning of the month that he was stingy with, but with his emotions, which he tended to hoard. He could not remember a time when he was in any way demonstrative, not even with his wife Hanan, with whom he felt he had shared nothing special for years. His two daughters were perhaps the exception, and even then only in those few moments he managed to carve out of a hectic work schedule. Only very occasionally was he unfaithful to his wife, the latest infidelity being with one of her friends, who often came to see them after her divorce from a colleague of his. Such was his caution and the studied mask he donned whenever necessary that he succeeded in keeping this relationship from Hanan for two years. She got wind of it by chance when she repeatedly smelled her husband on her friend's clothes and the woman's smell on her husband's skin. She kept watching them until she was certain, then she threw out the woman and forbade her from entering the house. For his part, he neither objected nor accepted, but ignored the whole thing until the storm had blown over. Afterward, he no longer had the patience to hunt a quarry and lay siege until he had her in his snares.

He woke up with a start and looked at his watch—he hadn't been asleep for more than ten minutes. He got up, despite a dizzy spell that forced him to shut his eyes, and snatched the suitcase on his way to the door. He was startled to see his wife, who had just come in with the girls.

"Were you going to leave without saying goodbye to us? I can't believe it!"

She gave him that smile that meant she wanted him. He had no time, though; he was worried about being late for the hospital, and the headache was bearing down on his temples. His older daughter, Mona, rushed into his arms and he dropped the suitcase and hugged her in turn.

"What do you mean? I was just getting ready. But of course I was waiting for you," he said to the three of them.

He sidled up to his wife and gazed into her eyes with what he hoped was an air of innocence. "I'm late. You know what hospital appointments are like," he murmured.

Hanan, who had had her head changed only three months earlier, exuded the vitality that follows the surgery, whereas he was "at the end of the line." For a moment he considered handing over the reins to her, and then decided to do just that on the spot.

"Let's have lunch quickly. I'll help you," he said.

Chuckling with pleasure because he could not resist her seductiveness, she whispered, "I'll take a bath. The food is ready, all you need to do is bring it out of the oven."

Hanan was late so the two girls decided to start eating as soon as their father set the food out. He sat quietly gulping down his lunch while they chattered incessantly. Each of the girls gave him a peck on the cheek then withdrew. The dizziness was mounting and the pressure on his temples was clouding his vision.

She came out in a bathrobe, water dripping off her hair onto her face so that her wide black eyes, with their look of feigned innocence, glistened. Going over to him she gazed at him quizzically, and he answered with his eyes.

"Oh, don't worry about it, in a week's time you'll be back with us," she said finally.

Noticing that he was overcome with fatigue, she murmured, "We'll go away on a holiday as soon as you're back."

He snatched his suitcase and stood in front of her. She pressed her whole body against his and kissed him gently. She was dazzling and radiated an intoxicating scent. Shutting his eyes, he backed out of the room. In an instant he had opened the door and was already on the staircase.

5

AGAINST MY WILL, I AM STILL STUCK to the iron bridge. Yet in those first few minutes in which I open my eyes seeking out the dew of dawn just before the merciless sun rises, in these very minutes lies what rest is to be had from the whole day. There is no pain whatsoever then, rather a mellow drowsiness, a languor, the slow opening of the eyes before they make out the details of the scene that has long arisen before me: fields that stretch out until hemmed in by the mountain's looming shadows over there, and here are the hills that every morning support the sun on their tips, while I receive it submissively.

Shuhdi Attiya al-Shafie

Attiya al-Shafie and his family announce the passing of their dearly beloved, the pride of youth, Mr. Shuhdi Attiya, whom they have lain in his final resting place. And to those who paid their condolences, they say: we shall not thank you, for to thank you would not do justice to your loyalty in this situation. It is to you that the memory of Shuhdi belongs, you are its guardians.

As for you, our dear departed, we eulogize you thus:

A youth who, stabbed with spear and sword, fell to a death
　　that bears the stamp of victory, though victory was not his.
Swathed he was in death's blood-red garments, but no sooner
　　had day dawned than they were the green silk of Paradise.
Easy it would have been to elude death, but it was
　the bitter dues of dignity and valor that drove him to face death.
A soul that shuns shame as though it were
　　a sin worse than heresy on the Day of Judgment.

Al-Ahram, June 20, 1960

Abd al-Hamid Haridi

Today, for the first time in more days than I can remember, they did not take us to do hard labor on the mountain. They usually made us carry from the ward to the mountain even those of us who would drop because of the regular feasts of torture prescribed all morning. Then we would divide among us the allotment of stones our companions were supposed to hew, which we carried in the reed baskets, as well as bringing back our companions with us at the end of the day.

Today, though, they did not let us out.

This could only mean one thing: that there were new "guests" assigned to arrive today or early tomorrow morning at the latest. We remained locked up in our cells until we overheard the voices of the jailers outside answering in indistinct words the commands of a row of officers who were themselves yelling. When, the following day, they had us vacate our cell and reallocated us to the rest of the cells, we ascertained that Cell Two had been set aside for the newcomers. We had discussed the situation the night before, and all the evidence indicated that these were the accused in the Shuhdi case in Alexandria.

We, the accused in the Fouad Mursi case, had already inaugurated the first "reception banquet" at the Abu Zaabal Prison Annex on November 17, 1959. Our first feast of torture took place during the two following days, when we arrived at Abu Zaabal Prison, presided over by Sergeant Hasan Mounir, the brutish chief warden who personally executed the whipping order on those thrown on the wooden "maiden." It was only two days later that the second reception banquet took place, when two hundred more prisoners from different organizations and cases arrived, which meant that the clampdown was expanding and hence that the torture would continue. It was the second reception banquet that witnessed the murder of Farid Haddad, the handsome doctor from Shubra, at the hands of the executioners who assaulted him while he was tied up with sticks and belts, until he breathed his last. He had not meant to provoke them, but then he was proud of his history as a Communist activist. As for Muhammad Mounir Mouwafi, the nationalist captain, they had a special reception for him after he was released from the Military Prison and beat him up when he was all alone at night so that he went a little crazy. Mouwafi had served as a liaison officer between the Free Officers' government and the battalions of Communist freedom fighters during the 1956 War in the Suez Canal zone. He was one of the most nationalist officers and the most loyal to Nasser.

So, it seemed this would be the fifth reception banquet, though the preparations for it were different and it looked like it would be a grand party—as befitted Shuhdi and his group.

Nur Sulayman

They'd packed the inmates of every three cells into a single van, and that was how I found myself in the same van as Shuhdi. When the convoy moved, we started chatting about this sudden transfer. Part of Shuhdi's speech for the defense in court, spoken on behalf of all the accused, argued that the government must take responsibility for our lives until the verdict was pronounced. This was because reports had reached us about the unrestrained brutality of the butchers who had surpassed their predecessors, the butchers of the monarchic period.

The first thing Shuhdi said in the van was that the fact that it was al-Halawani himself—the chief warden of Hadara Prison in Alexandria where we had spent the first months of our detention—who was handing us over to another prison was disquieting. We were therefore to expect a tough reception, whichever prison we were taken to. Despite the high esteem in which I held him, I couldn't help bursting out, "What I find hard to understand is how a nationalist government like President Nasser's would actually take it upon itself to sanction the torture, humiliation, wounding, and murder of Communist nationalists who stand by it. It was we in the Democratic Movement for National Liberation who printed their pamphlets back at the time when they were just a small organization. Then in the summer of 1952, which I will never forget, only two weeks after the Free Officers' coup, I myself took part in the efforts at conciliation during the strikes and sit-ins of the workers at Kafr al-Dawwar. Don't you remember, comrades? Do you, Shuhdi, remember when I asked to meet you urgently to point out that the Free Officers' having put to death the workers Mustafa Khamis and Muhammad al-Baqari had landed us in a quandary? Ignoring the issue in our propaganda was unacceptable, just as continuing to support the officers necessitated that they at least not kill the workers! That's if we wanted our propaganda to be consistent. You, Shuhdi, answered that we must not condemn Khamis and al-Baqari but rather defend them as wronged and condemn their execution. At the same time, we were to defend the nascent regime and also to go on showing up the conspiracy that targeted the Free Officers' movement in order to forge a rift between it and the workers. And we were also to persist in our call to shield the movement from its enemies who were primed to bring it down, more so after it got a grip on things and succeeded in expelling the king. You also said it was an exceedingly difficult task but that history would not forgive us the betrayal of the two innocent men whose blood had stained the hands of the movement. And here I say to you, Shuhdi, that the officers of this selfsame movement now torture and aim to liquidate us after the arrest campaign of the new year, which hardly spared any member of a Communist organization. This regardless of the differences between the organizations, some of which supported the Free Officers' movement that has now become a revolution—especially after the Bandung Declaration—as we in the Democratic Movement for National Liberation did, while others rejected it as a form of military Fascism, this being the position of the minority in the Communist movement."

"In any case," Shuhdi replied, addressing us all, "we should stand firm and face whatever lies ahead of us with utmost forbearance without succumbing to the provocations of the executioners." With a smile he gestured toward some of us who had caught the tail end of the monarchic period and the beginning of the Free Officers' era when prisoners were literally put in shackles. I knew that Shuhdi was among those who had undergone the shackling, but what exactly did he mean? Was he implying that our conditions now were better? I almost laughed outright. "History may lag until you get fed up," Shuhdi continued, "but in the end it progresses. It is no longer possible for any power to take history back to the pre-Bandung era. All over the world, a new movement has been born, the aims of which embrace dozens of anti-colonial and newly independent African and Asian peoples. Likewise, Nasser announced the nationalization of the Suez Canal and challenged the most arrogant and ruthless of imperial powers. We in turn stood by him, nor would it have been conceivable for us not to support him. None of the measures he took in the country could have been undertaken except by a nationalist government that we must back and support. The problem is that we need, simultaneously, to uphold our call for democracy, the annulment of martial law, and wresting our rights and the rights of all the political forces to independent organization."

I couldn't help losing my temper with Shuhdi as the van we were carted in rattled us while we sat spread out on its floor under patches of sunlight filtering through the narrow metal slits. "I'm a worker and not a theoretician like you," I said. "We've been supporting the regime for eight years, and the regime that we supported is now deliberately liquidating us. There can be no other meaning to what is happening. There are some who have in fact been killed: Dr. Farid Haddad, the medical doctor from Shubra and the finest of young men, is not the only one. Didn't the story reach us in Hadara Prison? He said to that dog, Younis Marei, 'I am an Egyptian Communist who believes in socialism.' Younis Marei answered, 'Oh, made in Russia, you son of a bitch?' And they dashed at him with the butts of their rifles. He screamed at Younis, 'You fascist dog!' And he spat at him before succumbing to a cudgel that fractured his skull so that he dropped dead. The prison doctor sullied his profession's oath when he wrote in his report that the death was of natural causes following heart failure. What can this mean? Is this not liquidation, murder?"

Appeasing my anger with his warm and charming smile, Shuhdi answered with his familiar gentleness, "What do you want then, Nur? Are we to denounce a nationalist government and call for its downfall? What would we say to people? True, we are against the government's militaristic inclination to arrogate exclusive power, and against the regime's executioners who incite it with all their might toward a rift with us."

There we were, rehearsing again the same talk we'd been going over ever since Shuhdi delivered his political plea at the Military Tribunal before the Lieutenant General Abdallah Hilal. He had, on the one hand, declared our support for the nationalist government and, on the other, held the court responsible for safeguarding our lives until sentencing. However, Lieutenant General Hilal did not take the trouble to respond and ignored the demand.

Where were we heading then? Where was the sluggish van headed in the midday inferno? As my companions fidgeted, the handcuffs clinked.

Abd al-Hamid Haridi

After they reallocated the comrades to different cells this morning, the jailer Eid, whom we dubbed "Blockhead," kept the six of us back. He instructed us on our task before rushing off and shutting the gate of the courtyard from without. We were to clean and water down that courtyard, which confirmed to me that there would be a grand beating in the presence of high-ranking officials and that they were certainly getting ready to receive other comrades, especially since they had redistributed us at dawn.

The six of us were from different cells even though we belonged to the same organization, the Egyptian Communist Party. But we hadn't had the opportunity to talk to each other in peace and without surveillance since we became the honored guests of Abu Zaabal Prison. The minute we woke up we'd run to the latrines as the jailers lashed at us. Each of us kept running non-stop while changing the urine bucket or answering a call of nature in the communal latrines. We were all barefoot and shaved down to the scalp, so that some of us didn't recognize the others. The jailers would get at the stragglers with their belts as we ran to line up in the row then started to intone after Officer Murgan, "Long live the United Arab Republic."

We intoned it three times after him then barely caught our breaths before we received the first feast of the daily walloping. Officer Murgan cheered, "Long live President Nasser."

Only a few people from the front rows repeated after him, following our leadership's instructions in order to protect our companions who were ill or weak. Then, suddenly, the entire prison force turned up, the soldiers and jailers having taken off their belts, some of them holding searing palm-leaf stalks, to begin the day's beating. I had no choice then but to keep running, driven to the mountain where we spent the day in the scorching heat cutting stones that we transported in reed baskets. The slightest delay meant a blow you could not avoid because you did not know which direction it might come from. Mounted on their high horses, the officers caught you in the back, while the soldiers got at you where you least expected it. After finishing our daily quota of work, each of us might, if it was his turn, carry out half a day's labor on behalf of a sick comrade or one whose health prevented him from getting to the mountain.

So we returned at the end of the day still barefoot, the soles of our feet torn from the stone slivers. On occasion, they'd force us to do more hard labor such as unload limestone blocks from train cars transported from the prison that were then stored at a distance from the railway.

This was why we'd hardly exchanged words before. But now the opportunity arose. I said to Farouk al-Qadi, who'd lost a lot of weight, "I expect it's the people from the Alexandria case who'll be the honored guests."

"Yes, but it seems a special reception will be held for them. A minute ago I heard the bugle. It must be that Himmat, that dog, will be attending in person."

That General Ismail Himmat, the director of the Prison Authority, was coming himself meant that they were going to be given a mighty walloping. Himmat attended only the grand receptions, and the officers and jailers would go to great lengths to prove to him that they performed their work with competence. It was Himmat, with his effeminate voice, sitting in the center, who had presided at our welcome reception. All he did was turn ever so slightly to the man sitting beside him, then raise his voice, "Make them look pretty! I want to hear each one of the boys saying 'I'm a bitch, a bitch.'"

Of course none of us would fulfill such a request, not even when submitting to the barber while receiving cudgel blows. I couldn't help smiling when this happened. Inwardly, I was perfectly willing to say I am a woman, but to say it to them—out of the question! Take me, for example: my wife Zaynab is stauncher and more stalwart than a hundred men. She shoulders the responsibility of the three children whenever I'm in prison, and for long periods at that. To withstand the beatings, I'd think of Zaynab and inwardly exclaim, "I'm a woman," without a word ever escaping my lips.

The following day, Captain Younis Marei passed by our ward, and went around asking each of us his name and occupation. When he reached Dr. Louis Awad, the prominent writer and academic, he asked for his name.

"Dr. Louis Awad," came the answer.

"A doctor in which field, son of a bitch? What do you do?"

"I am a counselor in the Ministry of Culture."

The captain hit him and ordered him to take a bucket to wipe the floor of the ward.

The six of us went about our work sluggishly, though we accomplished the required tasks with utmost care: when the jailers came back, they'd be at their most brutal after the tension and fatigue of the grand reception. We cleaned the courtyard well, and watered it too, while chatting about what would happen to our comrades who'd be arriving, and whom we had no means of helping in any way. After all that had happened, the members of the Democratic Movement for National Liberation, whom the prison was preparing to receive in grand style, still insisted that the regime was nationalist. They got beaten, dragged, and jailed, and still they went on saying it was a nationalist regime. I said to myself, even if Lenin had done what Nasser had, I wouldn't have hesitated to call Lenin a fascist. It had been eleven months that we'd been imprisoned and tortured every day. They sent us Ismail Himmat, who had specialized in torturing Communists since the days of the king, to undertake disciplining us himself. We were all now detainees. Whether sentenced or not, everyone was a detainee. Nasser put everyone in detention—all the organizations, even his sympathizers and the democrats, apart from the Communists, those of them who helped him and those who attacked him. He tortured everyone, including Captain Muhammad Mounir Mouwafi, whom I got to know in the days of the popular resistance in the Suez Canal back in 1956. He thought that they were going to kill him, and went hysterical, running around screaming, "Take me back to the Military Prison," though the stories we heard about it were even more terrifying. I saw him through the peephole of our cell running in circles in front of the jailers in the narrow space in which they'd cornered him while lashing at him with their belts. Even when he managed to break through the siege, one of the officers on horseback would get him with his whip.

Shortly afterward, Fouad Haddad wrote that poem that we all learned by heart and never tired of repeating:

I don't want day to dawn, people
don't want it to dawn, people.
I, human that I am,
they beat my father in me
beat my mother in me
there where my father kissed me
where my mother kissed me,
the beatings like insults
on your sore belly.
Why was it you carried me in your belly,

breastfed me your supper?
Why was it you called me by my name, mother,
when now they call me by a number
written on my blanket?
Why was it, mother, I learned to read—
went to school
and learned the alphabet?
For what the books and dictionaries,
the exams and feast money?
Why was it, mother, I
practiced my humanity?
Tell my father, who instilled
more than knowledge in me,
Abd al-Latif Rushdi has inherited
your son among his slaves,
Abd al-Latif Rushdi is his master,
Abd al-Latif Rushdi sits astride the government's horse,
an owl's ominous scowl drawn on his face.

The voices of the jailers were suddenly louder, reaching us from afar. The six of us went back to putting on a show of being engrossed in cleaning and watering. We hardly talked, though it was an opportunity not likely to be repeated, but then the welcome reception they seemed to be preparing for our comrades blotted out everything else from our minds. As the three of them—Eid the Blockhead, Abd al-Radi, and Corporal Abd al-Halim—came toward us they were covered in perspiration, their faces emitting evil sparks. Pointing at us, Corporal Abd al-Halim shouted, "Quick, put them in Cell Four."

Because I was standing on the opposite side, close to the observation room, the Blockhead hastily opened it and shoved me in. Then he went locked the door and left.

6

THIS TIME I WAS BEHEADED—and was it the last time?—without a single drop of blood, and it was to be the harshest and most painful of my beheadings. I was having one of my bouts of exasperation and weariness, my head being still stuck atop the iron bridge, facing the daily inferno that lasts from dawn to dusk when the flies disappear and the coolness of the night begins.

As for the story of my beheading without a single drop of blood, this suddenly sprang to mind during one of those episodes and saved me from going completely mad. It seemed I wouldn't be able to endure for much longer; time and again I was on the verge of losing my mind, and was saved only by recollecting what had befallen me in the past. But for how much longer would I have recourse to my memories? For how much longer would I be able to withstand? And why should I?

I did not remember that beheading, "clean and bloodless," directly; what first came to mind was a certain envelope that *roamed through so many countries, in the north and in the south, before finally reaching its destination.*

I t was on this small chair in front of Alia in the northerly room that had been her paternal aunt Iqbal's, overlooking the two slender minarets of the Muhammed Ali Mosque on the Citadel plateau, that the old manila envelope with edges torn from years of wandering was thrown. For about three months, the envelope lay in front of her. She would open it every day, at times to read her father Shaker's scenario about the nationalist leader Ahmad Urabi, at others to browse some of his notes that began in the first days of the invasion and left off close to the Iraqi border where all news of him got cut off, nor was it known even now in which land his head had finally come to rest.

It was not just the contents of the envelope that astonished and preoccupied her all this time. What fascinated her most was how it had changed hands among all those Iraqi artists and writers who had fled Saddam Hussein's regime to Scandinavian countries up in the far north, before reaching Alia at last, after a delay of some nine years during which it roamed several cities that did not include Cairo except at the end.

Nine years—what a long time the envelope had taken on its way to her!

In any case, there was the envelope lying in front of her. Her aunt Iqbal's name and address here in the Hilmiya district were written on it. As for Iqbal, she had committed suicide from this very terrace in a famous incident four years earlier. When the envelope reached Cairo, its bearer asked for Iqbal and was given the news. He then spent two years trying to return it to the sender, Abd al-Wahab al-Husayn in Denmark.

Abd al-Wahab al-Husayn was the brother of a soldier in the Iraqi army, Luai, who was part of the Republican Guard forces directly answerable to Saddam Hussein. Luai had got caught in the first air raids by the International Coalition forces when the harbingers of Operation Desert Storm were launched in the dawn hours of January 16, 1991, to level any cities along the way and raze them to the ground. As soon as the air raids abated somewhat he turned back with what remained of his regiment and dashed across the border. On his way he came upon dozens of corpses that had been overtaken by the air raids, but what caught his attention was a headless corpse of a plump man in civilian clothes, with a small green leather briefcase lying nearby. It may have been the color of the briefcase and its Andalusian print that struck him, so he bent down, picked it up, and tucked it into his jacket before forging ahead toward Iraq.

Back at home in Basra, Luai had ample time to open the briefcase and read Shaker's notes and his scenario for a film about Urabi. The passport he found in the bottom of the briefcase carried a picture that seemed quite odd to Luai, compared to the plump body without a head lying in the desert among a group of civilians following the incineration of a bus, the remnants of which still lay by the corpses scattered on the asphalt road.

Two years after the war, Luai's younger brother was getting ready to flee from a country that had been ruthlessly punished by the air, sea, and land forces of more than thirty nations, their rockets, poisonous gas, and chemical warfare representing the latest that the arsenals of the advanced west had produced.

Luai had already shown the contents of Shaker's briefcase to his brother Abd al-Wahab, a poet. He in turn was fascinated with Shaker's notes, which tailed off in early January 1991, just before his death. As for Shaker's scenario for a film about Urabi, this had been done on computer and seemed to be a final draft. When Abd al-Wahab passed it on to some of his friends who were cineastes, they were unanimous in their enthusiasm for the scenario which they designated as "avant-garde." But none of them had heard of Shaker, the name inscribed on the passport and various other documents, some of which bore the seal of the Iraqi government, others the Kuwaiti one.

When Abd al-Wahab decided to put his plan of escape into action he could not resist packing in the manila envelope with Shaker's papers, after taking Luai's permission. For a while, the envelope settled in Damascus, Abd al-Wahab's first destination, which he reached using a fake passport. There he met a Syrian film director who had studied in Egypt. As luck would have it, the director had met Shaker and Iqbal during his studies at the Cinema Institute in Cairo, and in fact he knew quite a bit about Shaker's long-gestating scenario about Urabi. When he saw the address on the passport, he urged Abd al-Wahab to send on the papers, whenever he had a chance, to Iqbal's address in Cairo, which he had recognized among Shaker's documents.

Abd al-Wahab got busy with the second stage of his plan involving his escape to the next destination, Switzerland. One of his Iraqi friends who had preceded him there was preparing to leave for Cairo, so Abd al-Wahab gave him the envelope to be delivered to Iqbal. He felt then that he had paid his dues by returning what he had been entrusted with to its owner, Iqbal, of whom his Syrian friend held the most cherished memories.

Abd al-Wahab's third and final destination was Denmark.

Two years passed before he got a telephone call from Switzerland in which the Iraqi friend whom he had given Shaker's envelope informed him that, on arrival in Cairo, he had found that the only topic of conversation among the capital's intellectuals was Iqbal's sudden suicide which had taken place only three days earlier. After a tour that lasted for some weeks, he had had to return to Switzerland, taking the envelope along with him. Abd al-Wahab asked him to forward the envelope to his new address in Denmark.

A while later, Abd al-Wahab decided to send the envelope by DHL to the same address, enclosing a note explaining how he had come by the papers and the reason for the delay of all these years. He also gave his telephone number and emphasized that he had no idea into whose hands the envelope would finally fall, especially now that he had learned of the passing of Mrs. Iqbal, but that he had resolved to make every attempt despite nine years having elapsed.

He was surprised to receive a phone call from Alia who wanted to thank him. He reiterated that he had learned about the sad demise of the late Iqbal, but that he felt that there must be someone who was more entitled to the papers than he was. She said that she was happy to be introduced to him and explained that she was one of two daughters of Shaker's, that she had graduated a year earlier from the English Department in the Faculty of Arts at Cairo University. Before she hung up, Abd al-Wahab asked for her phone number. He called her a week later and asked if she had read the papers. Alia replied tersely at first, and then found herself pouring her heart out about her father Shaker. She recounted how she had seen him crushed by her mother right after they returned from Qatar, where she had spent the larger part of her childhood, and how he had later turned cruel and violent when he lost his life savings in an Islamic investment company. Her mother had been very enthusiastic about the scheme and had more or less bullied him into depositing ten years' worth of savings in it, and then all was lost when the owner of the company decamped to Greece. Alia broke off to ask if Abd al-Wahab would like to correspond over e-mail. He said that he was about to make the same suggestion, though of course e-mailing shouldn't mean that they not call each other from time to time.

An unexpected warmth suffused his voice, so that Alia found herself admitting that the memory of her father arose vividly before her eyes when she read his scenario about the nationalist officer Ahmad Urabi's revolution. She'd decided, she said, to propose it to the film director Youssef Chahine, even force it on him if necessary, since he'd had a disagreement with her father more than a decade earlier, and she would remind him of her father and that incident too. She left off abruptly to say that talking to him was a real comfort. Finding she was unable to control her voice, she had a fit of embarrassed coughing. At the other end of the line, Abd al-Wahab was laughing delightedly. "Let's go on chatting over e-mail," he said. They quickly exchanged e-mail addresses.

Only a month into the e-mail exchanges between Alia and Abd al-Wahab, their relationship acquired a certain intimacy. He even called her once for five minutes and kept repeating that all he wanted was to hear her voice. For the next month, they exchanged long chatty messages every week, but soon this was no longer enough and they took to writing to each other on an almost daily basis.

Alia had just emerged from her second love story with her colleague Fouad al-Shafie which had lasted for the previous two years, and in fact they had come close to getting married. Their relationship had started when he came up to her one day and said that he had read her aunt Iqbal's book that had been published a few weeks after her suicide. Alia turned to him to see if she would recognize him. He said his name was Fouad—Fouad al-Shafie. "I graduated only last year, and I was told that you're my colleague here at the Faculty," he added.

Alia admitted to herself that it was Fouad who opened her eyes to the world so that she gave him everything, of her own accord and with a rare passion. He used to take her to Islamic Cairo, to the Gammaliya district where he introduced her to every nook and cranny of al-Muizz Street and showed her around the mosques, sabil water-houses, mansions, hammams, and wikala inn and trade complexes from Bab Zuwayla all the way to Bab al-Nasr. The only job he could find, and with difficulty at that, was to videotape weddings and birthdays at night, and in the morning he would carry a camera as they wandered together in the neighborhoods of the Citadel, Mari Girgis, Old Cairo, and the Muqattam Hills. Watching him whimsically snapping dozens of shots, Alia became infatuated. It was with Fouad that she visited the Museum of Modern Art and the Mahmoud Khalil Museum for the first time.

Their visit to the Mukhtar Museum reminded her of the week she had spent there with Iqbal. Her late aunt had taken her, her sister Dina, and a group of children to the museum where a professor of fine arts had undertaken an experiment to release the artistic potential of children. This was on the eve of the 1991 Gulf War. On the first day of the following week they found the Mukhtar Museum closed: a piece of paper pinned on the bulletin board carried an announcement that all activities had been suspended indefinitely and that all museums had been closed until further notice. She remembered the date clearly: January 16, 1991.

That week formed the subject of several messages Alia exchanged with Abd al-Wahab, because the memory of those days had come back to haunt him during an American air raid that destroyed several cities including Basra, his hometown where he had spent his childhood and early youth, leaving it only as a young man. She told him about a clay statue she had spent a week working on at the Mukhtar Museum, a statue of a palm tree, yes, a small palm tree. She'd been trying to fashion a little girl standing under the palm tree with her hand stretched out to reach for the dates, and it made her furious that she hadn't finished the statue. The children finally obeyed and turned back with their parents, leaving unfinished the project on which the art professor had staked so much. They slowly went down Qasr al-Nil Bridge, walking in the direction of the stone memorial plinth. In his next message Abd al-Wahab wrote that he felt he was about to lose his mind because the airplanes had destroyed, among so much else, the area he had been born in.

Alia noticed that the milk in the pan was about to boil over and spill onto the stove. She poured two cups of tea with milk at leisure for her mother and herself. She smiled inwardly as she reflected that her mother's health had much improved. Ever since her mother was diagnosed with uterine cancer two years earlier, Alia had been cooped up with her. Her mother had had a hysterectomy, but cancer attacked her lymphatic system so she was treated with chemotherapy. Alia watched her mother fade and shrivel to the point where she lost mobility, so that Alia could no longer leave the house unless she first called her grandmother Bahiya—that was before her passing—to ask her to come over and look after her mother while she was out. But in recent months her mother's health had picked up, and she regained control over her bowel movements; as for her urine, adult diapers absorbed it, and the bed would remain reasonably clean. Alia could now afford to go out from time to time, especially after her mother had recovered some of her lucidity.

She found her mother awake, her eyes gazing toward the door. Taking the tray to the bed, Alia said, "Good morning, Mom. How are you feeling?"

Habiba mumbled something with a smile and sat up in bed. She was gradually regaining her memory, her speech, and mobility, after the incremental dosages of radiation she had received for more than a year had debilitated her. But the physicians had affirmed that Habiba's present condition was a miracle by all standards and that her strong constitution had helped her withstand chemotherapy over prolonged periods, which was the only treatment possible in her case. This might be her mother's final year, Alia thought to herself; having to stay with her had been one of the reasons she withdrew from her relationship with Fouad al-Shafie. This despite her love for him, and indeed, whenever she remembered him, it was with a lovesickness that verged on grief, but then ever since she met him he had always been in such a rush. When they read together her Aunt Iqbal's book, it opened her eyes to that leftwing "ghetto" on the brink of extinction which had roped in, among others, Fouad and his cohort from the pot-smoking bohemia. Now, though, all that Alia wanted was a measure of peace and tranquility, and as little of the hustle and bustle of work and people as possible.

Fortunately, she was accepted at the bureau of the same Arab newspaper in which Iqbal had been employed. Thanks to her grandmother Bahiya's mediations before her sudden passing, after Alia's mother fell ill the editors allowed Alia to come into the office only to hand in translated material and receive the next installment. She became quite adept at her work, having received extensive training that started when she was in her final year as an undergraduate in the Faculty of Arts.

Her sister Dina had moved to Vancouver, Canada, on a fellowship to study cinema that she was awarded while still a first-year student at the Cinema Institute in Cairo. Alia still remembered the surprise Dina gave her and her mother when she announced that she had entered a competition and succeeded, despite stiff competition from two hundred students from different year groups in the institute, including those in the fourth and final year. Habiba could not bring herself to break the girl's heart, especially when Dina exclaimed, "As they say, 'He who has children will not die.' See how I take after my father?" For some time now Habiba had become altogether vulnerable to anything that had to do with the memory of Shaker. So Dina had left three years earlier, not returning even once. She would call them up every now and then, and was about to return when her mother fell ill, but then she wriggled out of it at the last minute.

Habiba's acquiescence to her daughter's resolve to travel to Canada was the beginning of a string of calamities for her. First, Alia wrested the right to stay out late, then Habiba ceased to receive the allowance for the girls' expenses that Shaker used to send, and afterward they lost all trace of him when the Gulf War broke out in 1991. But it was at that time that Ramzi, Shaker's brother, came to visit her in the apartment in the Madinet Nasr suburb, perhaps for the first time since she got married. He was generous, as was the wont of Shaker's people when death struck. Indeed, he was almost tender, whereas as a young woman she had never known him as other than sullen and aggressive—the ferocity with which he returned anyone's spite being proverbial in Shaker's family ever since she married him. "After Iqbal's death and Shaker's disappearance," Ramzi said, "and despite the fact that you and Shaker had already divorced when he left for Kuwait, there is no one more deserving of the Hilmiya apartment than his two daughters, which, as you know, has been fully paid for." He handed her the key to the apartment and added that he had in fact completed the procedure for the transfer of property, then gave her the title deeds. It was a god-send that solved all her problems. She sublet her apartment furnished in Madinet Nasr and moved with Alia to Hilmiya. It was not long before cancer struck and she had her uterus and ovaries removed. When she had a relapse she was treated with radiation therapy and her thick black hair fell out; she took sick leave from Saniya School where she worked as she was confined to the house. How it pained Alia to see her mother, who always thought of herself as a cut above everyone else, undergo all this. Her fastidiousness, refinement, and obsessive cleanliness, the vanity that she never missed a chance to vaunt—it all fell to pieces in the first months after she was diagnosed when she started the weekly radiation sessions.

Alia couldn't be sure her mother had in fact been saved, that the cancer was not temporarily in remission before the damn malignancy flared up again. But she did seem much better in the past year, thanks to Alia's total devotion and tender ministration.

Alia was still debating whether to show Habiba Shaker's papers. She knew only too well that her mother had continued to love him despite the divorce; when his disappearance lengthened, then his death confirmed, she changed completely. Habiba no longer had any compunction about accusing herself in front of her daughters of having caused all the calamities that had befallen them, and of being unworthy of a man like Shaker whom she had been responsible for losing. Alia sometimes thought that her father's papers that had reached her in that envelope might give Habiba some solace, but she always ended up changing her mind.

After they had had their tea with milk, Habiba made a sign with her eyes. Alia got up, propped up her mother against her, and walked her to the bathroom. Leaving her at the door, she returned and opened the window to get some fresh air into the stale room. She picked up the wet sheet, threw it by the bathroom door, and spread a fresh sheet on the bed. She tidied up here and there then went to the bathroom. She washed her mother, changed her clothes, and propped her up as they slowly proceeded to the living room now that Habiba could stay out of bed. Alia's biggest worry was that her mother should develop bedsores, so she was extra careful to keep her clean and make sure her clothes were dry all the time.

When Habiba had rested for a while in the Asyut-style armchair, she looked up at her daughter, "Find us a song on the radio, Alia."

Catching her breath, she tried to shift in her chair. As Alia went to the kitchen, the voice of Nagat, one of Habiba's favorite singers, flowed. She came back with a smile. "As luck would have it, Mom."

She hummed along with Nagat as she went about preparing their breakfast:

One day I woke
to the sound of a wedding:
I looked out of the window,
they waved to me and said:
'May you be next!'

Alia was a diehard fan of a certain generation of singers, the generation of Abd al-Halim Hafiz, Nagat, Shadia, and Fayza Ahmad, though also of their predecessor Abd al-Mittelib, and above all of Umm Kulthum. It was Fouad al-Shafie who introduced her to that generation with all the cassette recordings he gave her, one of which was of Nagat singing with Sheikh Zakariya Ahmad himself in the chorus. Alia held only the fondest memories of Fouad, but it had to be said that he'd always been so impatient. Ah well, the important thing now was that her mother should recover by some miracle. She might then be able to give up some of her duties at home and start going into the office. The managing editor was constantly badgering her to sort out her situation: this business of "working from home" had gone on for too long, as he put it.

After breakfast Alia switched on the computer and logged into her e-mail account, but there were no new messages. She thought of sending Abd al-Wahab a message, but changed her mind out of sheer boredom.

Part Two

ANOTHER MORNING LIKE EVERY OTHER MORNING, though I do not know why I recalled that my beheading in this sudden manner, which barely took a few seconds, is better than amputation, dismemberment, castration, and flaying, as happened to Muhammad ibn Abbada, who was captured in the days of Caliph al-Muatasim Billah, or to Ahmad ibn Abd al-Malik ibn Attash, commander of the Ismaili Citadel of Isfahan, who was skinned until he died and his body was stuffed with straw, or to the Damascene jurist Abu Bakr al-Nabulsi, whom Caliph Muatazz not only flayed and stuffed but also crucified.

My beheading in this manner is better, too, than what happened to Ibn Abi Naawas, one of the Qarmatian commanders: his teeth were extracted, then one of his hands was torn off by dint of having it tied to a spinning cog, then in the morning his other hand was severed together with his head and legs before he was crucified in the east of Baghdad. Better, too, than what befell al-Husayn ibn Zikrawayh the Qarmatian rebel, who received a hundred lashes before his hands and legs were severed and he was seared until he fainted, after which bits of wood were tied around his sides and belly and he was set on fire while the man just went on blinking.

Better, too, than what happened to Abd al-Hamid al-Katib, whom the police chief killed by heating a metal basin until it was glowing hot and putting it on his head. Or, for that matter, to the jurist Said ibn al-Musayyab, who refused to betroth his daughter to al-Walid, son of Caliph Abd al-Malik ibn Marawan, so the caliph gave orders to have him disciplined and he was flogged a hundred times on a cold day, then made to wear a woolen jibba before a jug full of water was poured on his head so he died a slow death. Or Khalid al-Qasri, who had been wali of Hijaz until Caliph Hisham ibn Abd al-Malik removed him for minor breaches and gave orders that a heavy cane be put on his feet which the executioners stood on top of until his feet bones broke, then they did the same with his legs, thighs, loins, chest, and head until he died.

As for the servant of the founder of the Qarmatian state, who murdered his master in the bathroom, his punishment was the gouging of his flesh with metal implements. Whenever Caliph Muatadid vented his wrath on one of his slave boys, a hole would be dug for him in which he would be dangled head first, then the hole would be stamped full of earth so that his soul would escape through his anus. Or the boy would be tied up, then his ears, nose, and mouth would be plugged with bits of cotton and pumps placed in his anus until it inflated and then it, too, was plugged with cotton. Then blood would be let from the two veins above his brow so that his soul would escape from this very spot.

These innovations must have afforded an unsurpassable pleasure to the executioners. For example, the bloodthirsty al-Hajjaj *could not restrain himself from masturbating as he spent most of his evenings watching his latest torture techniques and contraptions. In Andalusia, al-Muatamid ibn Abbad took such delight in contemplating the heads he had ordered hacked off that he had them planted in the garden of his house in place of flowers and fruit trees.*

1

As for the season of beheading of the "Master of Heaven's Youth," this started while Muslim ibn Aqil was hiding in Kufa to obtain the oath of allegiance from the people there to the son of the Prophet's daughter, al-Husayn, who had sent him for this purpose, and to prepare for the uprising of his followers. For his part, Yazid, the usurping caliph, being the son of his usurping father, got ready and took precautions. He gave instructions to two of the oldest and most competent employees in his private intelligence apparatus—Muslim ibn Said al-Hadrami and Umara ibn Uqba—to set out for Kufa and take charge of the "operation" targeting al-Husayn's followers. He also ordered the prince of Kufa, al-Nuaman ibn Bashir, to put himself at the disposal of these two emissaries. When Yazid sensed that al-Nuaman was procrastinating, he deposed him and had him replaced by Ubaydallah ibn Ziyad who had learned the lesson of his predecessor—more so as Yazid had mentioned in no uncertain terms that his first assignment was to arrest Muslim ibn Aqil immediately.

The various security apparatuses succeeded in picking up the trail and found the hub of the nascent insurgency in the Great Mosque. Ubaydallah charged a client of his from the Levant, Aqil, to make Kufa's Great Mosque the starting point of his search with the help of the sack of dirhams he had given him. Once Aqil had infiltrated al-Husayn's followers, he of course discovered Muslim's hiding place. True, Hani ibn al-Urwa's refusal to hand over Muslim, to whom he had given refuge, presented an obstacle. But Ubaydallah ordered him slain, thus launching the first season of beheadings.

With Hani ibn al-Urwa beheaded, Muslim ibn Aqil had no choice but to come out from hiding and accelerate the insurgency: he had on his side eighteen thousand men from whom he had obtained pacts and oaths of allegiance to al-Husayn. He immediately sent his messengers to them, and some gathered around the palace without any preparation. Ubaydallah ibn Ziyad's soldiers, who were ready for the battle, were well aware that rapid action and extreme cruelty would nip the rebellion in the bud, and hence the battle was over in no time. Soon enough al-Husayn's followers dispersed and abandoned Muslim who, by nightfall, found himself all alone. No one came to his rescue except for a woman standing at the door of her house waiting for her son, who took him in and kept his secret; however her son betrayed him and gave away his hideout.

So it was that Muslim ibn Aqil found himself in the hands of the henchmen of Ubaydallah ibn Ziyad, awaiting his death at any minute. Looking around him, he caught sight of Umar ibn Saad ibn Abi Waqas, which he saw as a good omen that lifted his spirits. Turning to Ubaydallah, he said, "If you intend to kill me, let me give my testament to Umar ibn Saad."

When Ubaydallah nodded his consent, Muslim went up to Umar and, drawing him aside, murmured, "Do you accept to take my testament?" Umar agreed, and Muslim promptly said, "Ask Ubaydallah to bestow my corpse on you, so that it will not be mutilated after I am killed." Dropping his voice further and leaning closer to Umar, he added, "Also dispatch a messenger to al-Husayn to let him know what has happened because of the treason of those who claim to be his loyal followers—the eighteen thousand men who had given their oath of allegiance to him—so that he should proceed to the Holy Sanctuary, Mecca, and reside there now that the truth about Kufa has been revealed."

Of course it would not have been proper for Umar—whose father had been the first to throw an arrow for the cause of God, and who was one of the ten to whom heaven had been pledged and the commander of the campaign that led to the conquest of Persia—to betray Muslim; yet this is precisely what happened. Umar divulged to Ubaydallah all that Muslim had entrusted him with. Soon enough Ubaydallah ordered Muslim to be taken to the roof of the emirate palace that hundreds had surrounded. The executioner struck his neck and his head rolled over before all the onlookers—for the season of beheadings had begun and heads were ripe for plucking.

That same day al-Husayn left Mecca paying no heed to Abdullah ibn Abbas who implored him not to make for Kufa whose people had in the past betrayed his father. Nor did al-Husayn take Abdallah ibn al-Zubayr's advice to make Mecca the base from which he would proceed after gathering his followers there. On his way to Iraq, al-Husayn met the renowned poet al-Farazdaq whom he asked, "How were the people when you left Iraq?" Al-Farazdaq answered, "When I left, their hearts were with you, their swords raised against you."

And yet al-Husayn forged on, meeting on his way many who tried to dissuade him though he still insisted on proceeding. On the outskirts of Kufa he learned of what had befallen his cousin and emissary Muslim and of his followers' betrayal. Looking around him, he found a thousand horsemen sent by Ubaydallah ibn Ziyad surrounding him. Al-Husayn went up to their commander, al-Hurr ibn Yazid al-Tamimi, and scattered before him two saddlebags full of letters from his followers, then turned back, heading for Hijaz. Al-Hurr caught up with him and stopped him saying that he had been ordered by Ubaydallah to seize him and bring him to the emirate palace. Al-Husayn had no choice but to proceed together with his people, all under arrest, until they reached Karbala. There they were stopped by a messenger who greeted al-Hurr but not al-Husayn, then handed the former a message that he read aloud:

> Have al-Husayn and his company stop at the spot where
> my message reaches you, and keep to the wilderness away
> from any trees or water source. I have commanded my
> messenger to inform me of what you have done. Peace be
> upon you.

This is how al-Husayn, having failed to return to Mecca, came to halt at Karbala. Al-Hurr turned to him firmly. "Do not give the emir something to hold against me. You are required to pledge allegiance to Yazid now. What do you say?"

"Your death would precede it," al-Husayn retorted.

"I received no order to kill you, but rather was commanded not to let you out of my sight until I have brought you to Kufa. Should you refuse, follow a route that does not take you to Kufa nor lead you back to Medina. I would then write to Ubaydallah ibn Ziyad or you could write to Yazid ibn Muawiya if you wish, or to Ubaydallah if you prefer, so that God may dispose of things in such a way that I will be innocent of whatever will befall you."

So al-Husayn and his people proceeded, with al-Hurr accompanying him. Turning to his people al-Husayn said, "Things have fallen out as you may see: the world has changed; it has turned against me and forsaken me, leaving only the vile. For behold, right does not hold sway and wrong is not forbidden. I see in death nothing but martyrdom for there can be no life among the iniquitous."

Al-Hurr turned to him firmly in front of the company. "Husayn, I pray you turn your mind to God, for I vow that if you fight you will be killed, and if you are fought you will die as I see it."

Al-Husayn turned to him mockingly, "Is it with death that you threaten me?"

They continued on their way to Uzayb al-Hijanat, where they met with four men coming toward them on their mounts, leading along a horse for their friend. Al-Husayn asked them, "How is it with the people you have left behind?"

The nearest one answered, "As for the notables, their bribes have greatly risen, and now that their purses are full, they are as one man against you; and as for the people in general, though their hearts lean toward you, tomorrow their swords will be raised against you."

Then he asked, "What happened to my messenger?"

"When Ubaydallah ibn Ziyad ordered him to curse you and your father publicly, he raised prayers for you and your father and cursed Ubaydallah and his father, and informed people of your coming and called for their support. Ubaydallah gave his order then and he was thrown down from the top of the palace."

Al-Husayn's eyes welled up and he could not hold back his tears.

2

WHEN THE FLIES' BUZZING AND STINGING DRIVES the pain to a pitch, I close my eyes and quickly latch onto one of the stories of my beheading to take refuge in my memories.

On the flight from the Gulf, I dozed off despite the coffees I kept bugging the skinny hostess to bring me. The weird thing was that I woke up erect from an erotic dream where I was having sex with the selfsame hostess with the taut hips. Catching sight of her pushing the food trolley, I gave her a smile of complicity and asked for another cup of coffee. She had to return my smile out of politeness.

Things had not been easy at all for me. I forgot the Dewey Decimal Classification and the Library of Congress Classification systems, as well as just about everything I'd learned at university and applied in my job as librarian at the ministry. I crawled on my belly, fawned on all and sundry, and toadied up even to the Pakistanis and Bangladeshis. I was always ready to do the locals any favor they asked for. For instance, during my first vacation in Cairo I met up, as arranged, with the two sons of Sheikh Fahd and their friends. I splurged on hospitality. I rented an apartment in the Mohandessin district for them, brought women all the way to their bedrooms, and showed them around the cabarets. They ate up half my vacation, but then I was certain I'd be duly repaid when I returned. Sure enough, after the vacation, they fell over themselves doing me favors and making my life easier.

Nor was it easy to earn such trust in a company as big as al-'Isa'i with its many branches staffed by people from all the races of the earth. The owner himself knew me by name and showed me special affection. I got promoted faster than any other employee and carried out my responsibilities to the utmost of my abilities. But I was never satisfied, and always came back for more. As for this heaviness that's been bearing down on my chest lately, I'm pretty sure I'll be over it in two or three weeks once I am back in my own country and with my family. What really worries me is that I almost lost my footing several times in the last two years. I no longer have the stamina to persevere in work with the same attention and obedience I've been known for through my years of service. My biggest fear is that the perseverance and competence with which I served strangers will quit me when it comes to my own project. It's true that my project is to open a mall like the many 'Isa'i branches and that I've therefore learned all the ropes and got the experience needed, but then there's this terrifying fatigue that verges on malaise which I can no longer ward off.

I expect Nagat will be able to shake me up and make me fit again. I certainly haven't begrudged her anything: I bought her a *collier* for two thousand dollars and my suitcases are packed with dresses and nightgowns and lingerie in every shape and color imaginable. I went shopping in the main center of our company and its branches to find lingerie sets in such brands as the hard-to-find British brand Mary Quant, and the French brands Nina Ricci and Valisere. For every day of the week, Nagat, you'll have a whole new set in different designs and colors—the gifts I brought this time surpass anything I gave you before. There's been a revolution in fashion so much so that even the bikini-style panties are out: panties are now down to a red embroidered flower right on the crotch with two strings wound around the hips, or a heart pierced with an arrow, or a dark strawberry, or a shiny silvery leaf.

I was brought back by the light touch of the hostess' hand on my arm urging me to fasten my seatbelt, which I promptly did. When we landed, I pushed ahead of everyone else. I made straight for the duty free stores and snatched not one, but two bottles of Chivas Regal together with four cartons of Marlboro Reds. Then I dashed to the arrivals lounge and picked up my suitcases from the conveyor belt and put them on a small metal pushcart. Shoving the cart amid the hustle and bustle, I looked up and caught sight of Nagat waving in the distance. I spotted Heba standing beside her and thought of rushing toward them but quickly restrained myself.

Here you are, Nagat, at last. I drew her to me and hugged her before remembering that Heba was waiting for her turn. Heba's embrace, though, was less warm.

"What's up, Heba girl?" I teased her. "No hug for your dad? Seems you didn't miss me, like we saw each other only yesterday, eh!"

I patted her on the cheek and kissed her again. The driver, Muhammad Saad, was standing around, and as I hastened to hug him too, I caught a whiff of the cheap Cologne 555 reeking from his face. I turned to Nagat, but she was looking away with Heba dragging her feet behind her. Muhammad was picking up two suitcases and I stopped him to ask about Dirbala, the customs clearance man. He reassured me Dirbala would be here in a minute and that I should wait while he went ahead with the suitcases to the car.

Before he went off Dirbala had turned up shouting loudly with that Suez Canal accent I loved. He gave me a cheery hug all the while chattering as I'd always known him to. He quickly went through the documents I gave him and said, "It'll go swimmingly, chief. Don't you worry now. Everything will be delivered to you, with a kiss on top of the deal, chief."

I left him to carry the remaining suitcases but he snatched them and insisted on walking me to the car. The Lada was parked in front of me. "I missed you, old girl," I thought, though I didn't like its condition. I looked at Muhammad out of the corner of my eye and decided I'd have it out with him later. Muhammad and I were soon done with fitting the suitcases onto the luggage rack and in the trunk. It was hot, but this was bearable Cairo heat not the hellish Gulf variety. I suddenly noticed that Ali wasn't with us.

"Where's Ali, Nagat?"

"He's gone to summer camp with the club. The whole swimming team from the club went to Ismailiya. They'll be back tomorrow in the late afternoon."

I settled in the front seat and stretched into it, then turned to her. "You mean he didn't know my arrival time?"

"Oh, we all do. He said to give you his greetings and to tell you he had to go to swimming training for just one single day."

The streets hadn't changed. The only thing was that there were more cars, the traffic was more congested, the smell of gasoline sharper, and the honking louder. I noticed Heba's silence; she'd hardly uttered a word since I arrived.

"I really missed you, Heba," I said as I leaned back toward her. "Haven't heard your voice in a long time. I brought a whole suitcase just for you—dresses and blouses and pants the likes of which even the girls in Europe haven't seen. The latest and smartest fashions in the world."

She forced a smile and I heard her muttering something. Heba's always been a quiet one. I don't recall that she ever took the initiative to speak to me on the phone. Every time I called, I had to badger Nagat, who in turn badgered Heba while I counted the minutes that would show on the phone bill as I overheard Nagat remonstrating with her. I turned again, just with my neck this time, to share a look of covert complicity with Nagat, and it amazed me to find her staring out of the window lost in thought. Before we devoured each other in bed we always exchanged looks of complicity that no one else could decode. Muhammad broke the silence, saying, "Thank God for your safe return, Hajj."

"And may He keep you safe, Muhammad," I replied, gritting my teeth. "But I don't like the condition of the Lada. I bought it brand new, Muhammad."

"It was brand new four years ago, Hajj. Anyway, it's due for an overhaul. It'll go through technical inspection by the Traffic Authority in two months' time."

"Oh well, we'll just have to wait and see. Anyway, this time I'm here to stay, and won't be traveling again."

I looked at Heba again. "Heba, darling. Every time I'm back after a few years abroad I find the place overrun with flyovers and bridges."

I smiled and gazed into her eyes. They were not as transparent as they used to be. Lurking in them was this obscure anxiety that weighs on girls when they blossom into pretty young women like Heba and start sharing secrets with their mothers. But then I was startled to hear her say, "It's not just the bridges, Dad."

"What else, my philosopher?" I broke in laughingly.

She didn't reply so I turned again while we were getting off October Flyover in the direction of Doqqi. When I first left, Heba was six years old. During the year she spent in kindergarten I was the one who picked her up, after taking permission to leave early from the ministry library, to bring her back to our apartment in Boulaq al-Dakrur. Looking out of the car window, I caught sight of the parapet of her old school in Doqqi in front of me. I almost reminded her of the school and Miss Sahar, her young teacher whom Heba grew attached to as if she was her mother. Nagat used to pass by the nearby kindergarten on her way back from the Ministry of Supplies where she worked to fetch Ali, who was only three years old and couldn't be parted from her. What days those were, with my family in Naga Hammadi and hers in Suez. I'd been introduced to Nagat by my friend Hamid and his wife in their house in Rawd al-Farag. We visited her family once to speak to her father about the marriage and recite the opening verse of the Qur'an to seal the agreement, which was followed by another visit in which I married her before we returned together to Boulaq al-Dakrur. We got so busy after Nagat had our first child that we never had the time to visit my family in Naga Hammadi. I suddenly felt dejected when I remembered my father, only now, though I hadn't seen him for ten years. And my mother, how's she doing? I heard that my two brothers Husayn and Fathi were somewhere in the Gulf too, while my sisters Fatima and Zaynab were both married and living near Naga Hammadi the last I knew of them ten years ago. What days those were. As for Nagat, I don't remember her once asking that we visit Suez. After we got married, I learned from my friend Hamid—incidentally, I must visit him this time. Every time I return on vacation I remember Hamid and plan to visit him, then I always forget. But this time isn't a vacation;

I'm back to stay and can easily carve out an hour to go to Rawd al-Farag as soon as we're back from Alexandria. But what reminded me of Hamid? What about him? Oh, it was Hamid who told me that the dolled up old woman I thought was my mother-in-law and whom I didn't trust from the minute I first laid eyes on her swaying her hips as she brought us sherbet in Suez was not Nagat's mother but her stepmother. After we got married, Nagat didn't even bother to answer whenever I quizzed her about her relationship with this woman. Did she love her or hate her? Why did she never mention her, and why did she avoid talking about her family? Nagat either remained silent or changed the subject, so much so that I've now forgotten my mother-in-law's name. What was even stranger is that none of her relatives ever contacted us; in fact, I can barely remember her brothers. Oh, now it comes back to me: I think her brother Mamdouh once passed by me in the ministry to certify some document for him, I forget what, with the government stamp. When I mentioned it to Nagat at the time, she didn't comment, as usual. Mamdouh didn't even ask out of politeness for our address when I invited him to lunch. He refused the invitation, saying he had several errands to run, and I insisted that he stay with us while in Cairo and that his sister's house should take precedence in offering him hospitality. Since that day, I haven't seen him once, nor did I see any of Nagat's other relatives. We'll reach the house by 4 p.m. as I figured yesterday evening while packing. I should first stop by Ibrahim al-Ghul's café at the beginning of Faysal Street to stock up before heading home. I had it all worked out with al-Ghul in advance. I'd called up my friend Ismail and asked him to pass by al-Ghul and have him prepare a large chunk of hash and a small piece of opium, extra quality—the expense was no object, the quality of the stuff was the thing.

Muhammad turned at the university then swung onto Sudan Street. At the top of Faysal Street I said to him, "Turn right here, Muhammad, and now left, just here. Down this alley, and now stop right here." I leaned back and said to Nagat, "Just half an hour. It's a small errand, Nagat. I'll be back by the time Muhammad has brought the suitcases upstairs."

I rushed down the intersecting alleys drenched in sweat. I soon got out of breath and had to slow down. I must've put on a lot of weight; no doubt I've become a fat old man. It's true I used to notice, in the seconds I snatched in front of the mirror combing my few tufts of hair across the expanding bald patch, that I'd put on weight. But I never imagined I'd grown so heavy that the slightest exertion would make me sweat so much. Al-Ghul caught sight of me from afar and got up beaming and laughing.

"Thank God for your safe return, Hajj. Welcome to those who have come from the land of the beloved Prophet."

We hugged each other then sat on two chairs on the street corner.

"I missed you, Ghul. But first, let me give you this—a whiff from the land of the Prophet." Thrusting my hand into my pocket, I brought out the amber string of prayer beads and the bottle of Prophecy cologne and said, "I'm dying for it, brother."

"Let's have tea first," he broke in. "Mr. Ismail told me, and I've got it right here in my pocket."

"Make it extra fine, Ghul."

"Extra it is, Hajj."

His torso leaning back, he called out, "Fetch us some tea, boy, special miza tea, no boiling now."

I pulled off the cellophane wrapping around the opium. Just from its rich darkness and oily sheen, I could tell, even before biting off the tip to put under my tongue, that it really was extra grade.

I let its tangy bitterness roll over my tongue, and sat back enjoying the cool breeze wafting toward us, while the boy set the tea and the waterpipe's clay holders for the coal and honeyed tobacco in front of us. I went on chewing off little mouthfuls of hash then placing each bit—my signature, as I liked to think of it—on a coal holder. In the wink of an eye, I had graced twenty coal holders with my signature. I'd tear off a bit from the large lump of hash, relishing that I had the whole of it in the palm of my hand, then roll what I'd bitten off between thumb and pointer into a little disc that almost covered the tobacco on the holders. I looked up to find al-Ghul chuckling merrily, his swarthy face lighting up.

"Mr. Ismail told me you'd be arriving today. Is it true you just got back?"

"I came straight from the airport, haven't even gone home yet."

We burst out laughing hard. Even the boy who was bringing us drinks laughed and said, "Thank God for your safe return, Hajj."

It was that mellow, expansive mood I always went into with the first ten batches of hash. I wordlessly stretched out my hand with a whole pound to the boy. He was overjoyed and went off to change the water in the waterpipe. In front of me were remnants of agricultural land, now reduced to a few scattered patches encroached on by dozens of buildings propped up against each other, forging narrow winding alleys between them. I was unable to see beyond the stunted, misshapen houses that crowded the skyline and blocked the horizon.

"What's all this, Ghul? I was here only three years ago. Your neighborhood was all greenery and fresh air and fields and even cattle. There was so much space around you."

"Guess how much a square meter of this dirt costs, Hajj? Right here in this neighborhood it comes to more than a hundred pounds, and the prices are still going up."

The boy came back carrying a sparkling clean waterpipe, smelling of detergent and with water dripping off it. The glass flask was frosty, which meant that the water was nicely chilled. I tackled it eagerly and finished it off almost in one drag. The coals crackled, burning orange and splintering here and there. I handed the waterpipe to al-Ghul who said, "You're doing great, Hajj. You'll set the house on fire in a minute!"

I felt myself soaring into skies that opened to receive me. The opium made me alert and energetic while the hash slowly suffused my body. We were hard at it silently until we had finished off the waterpipe refills. The boy had the water changed and I placed my signature on twenty coal holders. Al-Ghul contented himself with ordering two lightly sugared Turkish coffees for us. I got really high and just kept soaring. I found myself light and relaxed as my head slipped out of my control and took leave of me. But then I felt ecstatic that it had separated from me.

Al-Ghul, meanwhile, was just as I'd left him: a discreet, polite, and stalwart local guy capable of protecting his customers from police raids. When the stuff is so good, this is what it does to you: the intense concentration while being spaced out, the lightness of being, the restrained daring, and the courtesy. My thoughts turned to Nagat and I almost got an erection, so I decided it was time to leave. As I expected, al-Ghul refused to let me settle the bill for the drinks and tobacco.

"For shame, Hajj," he said in a low voice. "Let me take this, it's the least I can do. You've always been so generous."

3

SUCH A LONG DAY IT WAS that I was destined to live through, while still a boy, amid the demonstrations of the indigent in the streets of Cairo. I recalled that day while forced to stare in front of me with the sun relentlessly progressing to plunge me into its inferno. I recalled it as I watched the schoolboys waiting on the station platform for the train that would take them to school. The girls, too, stood around in groups chattering and laughing, their voices chirping in the early morning.

On that long day, the gutsiest people I saw were the ones who tried to tear down the gate of the Sayyida Zaynab Police Station, afraid of no one. When the shooting broke out and I caught sight of the man beside me breaking into a run while holding up his bloodied arm which looked like it was about to come off, I dragged Umar by the hand. We ran for all we were worth until my feet bumped into the tram rails. I realized then that we'd covered the length of Port Said Street and reached

Ahmad Mahir Hospital. With the gunshots echoing in the distance we went on running past the National Security Authority building which was surrounded by hundreds of armed soldiers and totally secured by armored cars on all sides. We paid no attention and surged forward with everyone else. When we got to al-Azhar Street we paused at the intersection, waiting for the smaller bands of demonstrators coming in from all directions to flow together into one united mass headed for Ataba. Everyone was chanting in unison after a man carried on their shoulders:

You who rule us through your secret police
Everyone knows about your injustice.

With so many people in the demonstration, there were different groups each chanting after a leader. The three of us—Umar, Nagi, and myself—were at a loss as to whom to follow, each slogan being stronger and more hard-hitting than the other. It seemed that the last shred of fear had gone, to the extent that the slogans referred to Sadat in Abdin Palace:

You who rule us from Abdin
"In the name of justice and religion"—
Where is justice, where religion?

The following band of demonstrators also addressed Sadat:
Tell the sleeper in the palace
The workers sleep on empty stomachs.

Why was I feeling so warm? Was it because of all the running we'd done? Or was it the chanting with all our might following the men and young guys carried on people's shoulders? Or maybe the breaking away from school and home and my dad who's scared of everything? My ear picked out the slogan I liked most and I joined the next band of demonstrators intoning it:

They eat chickens and swig whisky
While hunger makes us dizzy.

What would my dad do if he saw me chanting anti-government slogans and cursing the president and the police? Whenever he's alone with my mom, I overhear him unburdening his fears while she soothes him, saying my sister Maryam would soon be graduating, and that in a year's time he wouldn't have to worry about her anymore.

"Fire! Fire!" Nagi screamed. He pulled me by the hand, and I pulled Umar in turn. I looked in the direction Nagi had pointed and saw the first floor of the casino opposite Ibrahim Pasha's equestrian statue aflame. If it was the non-stop running that saved us from the bullets, I was thinking, then run we must to escape the fire. We crossed the square together, headed for the downtown streets. After a few minutes, we stopped and Umar took out his pack of Cleopatras and offered each of us a cigarette. While we were puffing away Umar leaned over and said, "The demonstrations are growing by the minute. Looks like we won't be going home anytime today."

"Even if we try," I answered, "there are demonstrations all over the place."

Nagi was the oldest among us; he'd flunked and repeated a year in primary school, then another in middle school. Because his father beat him, his mother was very protective, and would give him plenty of pocket money behind his dad's back. He could afford to buy a whole pack of cigarettes and show off in front of us. And here we were, Umar and I, taking turns offering him our cigarettes since he'd forgotten his handbag with his money, cigarettes, and sandwiches on the bus. When we were done, we caught up with a small group of demonstrators, and Nagi and I helped a boy up on our shoulders. The boy chanted:

Parliament's all cronyism and spin
While people's freedom is reined in.

Not only did we keep chanting back the slogan, we didn't put him down until there were only the three of us left. Everyone else was running toward Tahrir Square, though we hadn't seen a single soldier since the massacre in front of Sayyida Zaynab Police Station. When we finally made it to the square, the sun's rays were filtering only intermittently through the clouds, though it was midday. The clock on the Arab League building showed 2:00 p.m. The smell of tear gas was so overpowering I reckoned it meant there were soldiers lying in wait nearby. Soon enough rows of soldiers did in fact appear, blocking the entrances to Garden City with its embassies and classy residences from the old feudal aristocracy. I spotted them in their helmets as they gripped their machine guns, and when they started firing in the direction of the demonstrators there was complete chaos. At first, I let myself go with the pressure of the crowd, but at the last minute I managed to catch Umar by the hand and we ran with everyone else. We crossed Qasr al-Nil Bridge and walked toward al-Gazira to cross the smaller bridge. I turned to Umar in fear, and it scared me more that he turned to me just then. Had we lost Nagi? We went in different directions calling out to him then turned back, paced up and down, and called him again, but it was no use. Nagi had melted into the crowd.

"Take it easy," Umar said. "Nagi's a clever rascal, in a minute he'll be coming along and cadging a cigarette."

"Where should we go, Umar?" I asked after we'd walked for a while.

"No problem. How about stopping just here by the Nile to have a bite? Can't leave Nagi, now. He may be a while joining us, so let's just wait."

I nodded. The pale sun had moved to the center of the sky and it was obvious there wasn't going to be any trip. But there was nothing to stop me from spending the day as I liked and going home just before nightfall. No punishment from my dad, no holds barred. It was the same story two years ago when I was a pupil in the Ahmad Mahir Middle School and had signed up for a trip to Hilwan. Demonstrations swept the town that day, so the driver took us back to school. I spent the entire day with my friends amid the demonstrations, but they were much smaller, and things didn't reach the extent of buildings being set on fire. This time, it looked like all of Cairo had turned out for the demonstrations.

There was a small kiosk across the street with people clustering around it. I went over when I was done eating and had wrapped up the remaining sandwiches and put them in my empty handbag. No punishment, no holds barred, I thought to myself as I bought two Ica chocolate bars and a small pack of Cleopatras. I crossed back and gave Umar one of the chocolate bars, then we crossed over again, headed this time for the square. I was startled to see rows of soldiers on the street corner by the hotel. The street was littered with them in their black uniforms, wielding batons and shields, their faces hidden behind helmets. Huge black vans also occupied the street corners with machine guns pointed at the square. I suddenly remembered that Sadat, whom all these demonstrators were heaping invective on, lived right there, behind the girls' school, and realized why the place was chock-full of soldiers and armored vehicles.

When the avalanche of stones hurled from the square toward the soldiers started, they received them in silence, until the first rows of people drew up close. Then the soldiers battered them with their batons and shields, while the stinging odor intensified. It was as if they'd set everything on fire with their tear bombs. I felt nauseous and my eyes watered. I glimpsed Umar's hand beside me and gripped it, then we started running together searching for an escape.

We finally got through, and I realized that they wouldn't let anyone even approach Sadat's house. In any case, we had to get away immediately. The two of us went running down side streets with other people but soldiers kept turning up from every direction. It was another massacre that nothing could stop. People were screaming as they dropped, but no one paid any attention to them. There was so much pressure on all sides that I lost my grip on Umar and he fell to the ground. I eased myself down, leaning on my forearms, then released one of them to pull up Umar by the shirt collar. I was relieved that he responded to my tugging. I finally managed to find an outlet for us. We crossed a square, with me still dragging him, then a garden. At last, the familiar dome of Cairo University, at which my sister Maryam was studying, loomed radiant in the pale sunlight.

We saw no soldiers around, just people catching their breath and chatting.

"You came within an inch of your life, and so stupidly," I said.

He gave me a dazed look and didn't answer for a minute then glanced away as he said, "Well, thank God we're alright now."

Umar handed me a cigarette and lit it up for me. I had hardly ever smoked as many cigarettes as I had that day, and started coughing and Umar joined in. Soon we were both coughing uncontrollably until people started staring at us and we stopped. I thought of my brother Hatim, who was the only one who knew I smoked. He was three years younger, and yet he often got away with extorting things from me. All he needed to do was wave this card in my face, threatening to let my dad in on my secret, especially when we were going to share things among us. My sister Maryam, though, had her own room where she spent most of her time trying out different hairstyles and listening to Abd al-Halim Hafiz tapes playing nonstop on her cassette recorder.

Life was beautiful just then, with no soldiers in sight. I stamped out my cigarette and turned to Umar. "What do you say we go to the Pyramids?"

"The Pyramids? How would we get there without transport?"

"We'll walk. No problem, as you say. We're quite close, you know."

The demonstrations hadn't petered out. As soon as we'd crossed to walk along the campus parapet, row upon row of demonstrators passed beside us. The bigger group of demonstrators was following a young man with a blue scarf around his neck. Carried on the demonstrators' shoulders, he was chanting something I didn't catch, though it was directed against Israel occupying our land. The next demonstration was all invectives against Sadat. One group of demonstrators followed another as we walked along the parapet of the zoo until we reached the big square. We crossed the tunnel, and stopped for a while on Pyramids Road, just before the small canal. Umar seemed dead tired as he stood there panting and looking at me. He'd been chanting slogans all the time, and his face was flushed with sweat running down his forehead and temples. We leaned against the embankment of the canal and I brought out the pack of sandwiches, which were really mushy crumbs by now. I picked out for him the bigger bits of bread and whatever leftover filling my fingers came across. He'd lost his bag with the sandwiches in it, just as we'd lost Nagi earlier.

"We're hungry, and this food won't keep us going," he finally said. "The minute we find a restaurant, let's stop and buy food. It's no problem, I have money on me. My dad gave me fifteen pounds first thing in the morning. But where's Nagi? We've lost him, haven't we?"

We finished eating shortly, and took a few steps. But then we were so dead tired we had to stop again and sat down on the parapet of the bridge over the small canal. My body was aching all over and Umar too was breathing with difficulty as he watched the street. I took the pack of Cleopatras out of my pocket and we lit up. The cigarette tasted good and made me drowsy all over in no time. I felt my eyes drooping but Umar tapped me on the forehead just then.

"Don't tell me you're going to doze off here! It's a revolution out there. Get up now!"

We helped each other up. I saw the splinters of glass from the smashed ads on the lampposts piled up here and there. Most of the store windows on either side of the street had been shattered, but there was one fuul bean restaurant that was open with people crowding in front of it. Umar went in ahead of me and returned in a minute looking cheerful. "Sizzling hot felafel."

We went and sat on the pavement this time. The sun had moved to the other side of the sky and no longer gave off warmth, but just tinted everything yellow. I thought of my sister Maryam who was the only one to defend me whenever I was late; my mother couldn't stand up to my dad when he had a fit of temper.

"What do you mean, let's go to the Pyramids?" Umar said suddenly as he leaned over. "We should just go home. This is bigger than we thought, it's a revolution. Where's it all going to take us?"

I ate the last morsel and got up hastily. "Well, let's just walk on and see what happens. Who cares about the Pyramids, and who cares about the revolution? We'll just go with the flow."

He pulled me by the hand. "Okay, no problem. Let's get something to drink."

There was a kiosk on the opposite side of the street. I beat Umar to it and brought back two bottles of Coca-Cola. Mine was lukewarm, but I was suddenly feeling parched and downed it all in one gulp.

4

IN THE DAYS IMMEDIATELY FOLLOWING the accident that hurled my head atop the iron bridge while I lost control over my limbs and my body staggered, people would often stop to stare. Students, government functionaries, workers, girls blossoming into their first love stories, pubescent boys with croaky voices—all stood around narrating different versions of the accident. For a little while, the stories they exchanged about me kept me entertained, but they soon enough lost interest in me, especially after the village managed to get rid of my body, which was shipped to town for burial, leaving only my wide-eyed head stuck to the iron bridge. The loss of control over my limbs and the headless staggering had been altogether humiliating, so that after my body was buried, things seemed somewhat more bearable.

Having said goodbye to his wife and two daughters, he went on his way before noon and hailed the first cab he saw. When he got inside, he felt that heavy sense of depression akin to fear closing in on him. It would be only a week anyway before he could start anew. As he gazed out of the window, he remembered how it always began: the loss of control over his limbs, his actions outstripping his intentions, the blundering through utterly familiar things like avoiding the broken last step at the entrance to the house or ducking slightly in the narrow hall that adjoined his subordinates' office, and his marital relations going slightly awry. But now everything would finally be disciplined and regulated.

He got off in front of the hospital and walked toward the door awash in mild winter sun. He brought out his magnetic ID card and handed it to the doorman, then went in submissively. As soon as he entered the first room, they started working on him. They stretched him out on the table, took the various samples, measurements, and x-rays needed, then anaesthetized and decapitated him. Before he came to they sutured the wound and went on with their work, preparing the drips to feed him intravenously. No sooner had they removed his head than they got on with their work vigorously. They promptly started working on his larynx and vocal cords, his armpits and specs, and then turned to some of his glands. Finally, they took him out to the intensive care unit. The head would be sent to a special department located in the main building of the hospital surrounded by dense fruit trees, though these could not disguise the odor of human flesh. It was there that the head would be shaved before it was opened and prepared, then delivered to specialists who would download programs on diskettes to be inserted into the designated slots, as well as scan the various brain centers for any parts that needed replacement. As soon as the body came to in the intensive care unit it would be taken to the ward. He relaxed on the bed they had stretched him out on, and as he tried to regain control over his limbs he felt extremely debilitated, almost on the verge of death.

The following morning he was up and about. He managed to recognize the sorts of voices that escape through apertures above the middle of the neck used for breathing. Remnants of memory synchronized with habits imprinted on his organs enabled him to handle things and even exchange a few sentences with his ward companions. He would be injected with drips every morning then left to himself until five in the afternoon. As soon as they were done injecting him, he would start gravitating toward what seemed to be a wide terrace. Through his breathing apertures he smelled an odor that was so repugnant to his body that it nearly refused him and turned back, but just then the hint of a tune in the distance caught his bemused attention. His body was constantly trying to resist the temptations of adventures that beckoned whenever the remnants of his memory, which usually kept him in check, gave way. On the first day, the nurse rinsed him after he had defecated, then took him for a short walk; when she had him take a turn he sensed her body pressing him to the wall. About to fall over, he clung to her shoulder, and in those few seconds his hands rubbed and squeezed her breasts fervently. It seemed to him that she had abandoned herself to him and he went on pressing her to the wall. She caught him by surprise with a strong shove that banged him into the opposite wall so that he dropped to the ground. He decided to let himself fall in front of her. Through the two breathing apertures at the base of his severed neck he tried to cry out as loudly as he could muster, but they had anaesthetized his vocal cords as a precautionary measure undertaken with everyone who was admitted into this hospital that exclusively offered this advanced service. He realized shortly afterward that the nurse had left him and gone on her way, no doubt as a punishment.

It was adventures such as this when he broke free of what remained of his memory that excited and egged him on. He got up with his hands stretched out until he had touched the opposite wall then he turned along with the corridor and covered the remaining stretch without a problem. He picked out the smell of the terrace—that odor of human flesh mixed with the scent of fruit trees—and wended his way toward it. There was the iron railing of the terrace with its cold feel. When his body collided with another body he braced himself for another escapade. He nearly toppled but propped himself up by clinging to the terrace railing. It came to him just then that whomever he had bumped into had risked an even bigger fall, which could only mean that that person was likewise headless. He pulled himself together and tried to summon the traces of his memory that his body stored, which would come to his rescue in the remaining days. After the first three days at the hospital, when his body would have lost those memory traces, he had to surrender to the doctors and nurses completely so that they could have their way with him until they brought back his head and started to revive his brain. The first weeks afterward were always euphoric by dint of the wild recklessness and unrestrained whimsicality that overtook him. But he would soon become disciplined and things would go as they should. He was sure he would be rid of the loud din that had pounded in his head sometimes for as long as two years, and that his relationship with his wife and daughters would be back on track. On previous occasions when he had undergone the periodical maintenance procedure, he would throw himself afterward into the joys of conjugal life, and take his wife and daughters on evening outings at the club. On one occasion he even took them on a short vacation at a seaside town whose hotels he frequented. He contented himself with staying in, raptly watching the rain falling outside, while he sipped wine behind the wide windowpanes fashioned after an architectural style dating back more than a century. He would then spend some time chasing a woman with utmost care, except that his painstaking siege more often than not came to naught. In fact, in one of these attempts, after he had cautiously cast his snares for two months, and just when he was expecting to catch the quarry, she met one of his friends by chance, while out with him, and slept with the man that very same night.

His limbs obeyed him and he got up. He took a few steps until he had reached the iron railing and gripped it, then stood silently. He decided to wander around aimlessly—in any case, if he lost his direction, they would take care of bringing him back through the magnetic card attached to the front of the hospital gown. He went wherever his feet led him, ambling slowly with his hands in his pockets. Bumping again and again into others, he took to stretching out his elbows as far as he could to avoid toppling over. When a little later he went down a staircase, he started enjoying the game. He went on strutting down the staircase without losing his balance.

He kept going down passageways and corridors, colliding every now and then with others, sometimes so forcefully he would be thrown to the ground. But when these others went on their way and he realized that no one would come to his aid, he could not resist getting up and walking on. He went down a staircase then came across another staircase going up and he could not resist bounding up it. He broke with inhibitions and followed his impulse to run. He went running and picked up speed as he bounded across several flights of steps with successive leaps until he bumped into a closed door and crumpled beside it.

The next day, they kept him tied up all morning after two sturdy nurses had brought him back from the toilet, injected him with a strong sedative, then left him. He was sedated again the following day, as they had tried to set his bones with splints in different spots, but his ankle was fractured so they made a special cast for it from a metal that secretes a substance that promotes healing. They asked to see him the following day. Two male nurses wheeled him on his bed to the main building. He returned the same day in the evening complete with his head, though he was, of course, unconscious.

5

A LABYRINTH. I WAS BEHEADED so many times that the details got jumbled up and became a veritable labyrinth. Every time, the difficulty lies in settling on a starting point to distract myself from the gnawing of the flies and the daily blaze of the sun. It was no easy matter to hack off a head, nor would any of these heads have voluntarily submitted to the blade. The heads got jumbled up and I lost the threads of their stories that I once had a grip on and which would come back to me every morning.

Suddenly I remembered—with what delight!—my favorite story in Abu Zaabal Prison.

Saad al-Din Abd al-Mitaal

At last, the van in which they were carting us from Hadara Prison in Alexandria came to a standstill. Those who were asleep woke up and started fidgeting. I had been wanting to urinate even before we got ready to leave. But they had given us only a few minutes that were barely enough to burn some important documents. What caught my attention from the start was that Chief Warden al-Halawani was accompanying us. We had gotten used to being transferred from one prison to another, but this was probably the first time that a chief warden accompanied the prisoners transferred from his prison.

On this trip to an unknown destination, we went on discussing the matter. Where were they taking us? And why was al-Halawani accompanying us? And was this related to the fact that we had been tried and were awaiting sentencing? Shuhdi, whose opinion would have helped us predict what would happen, was not with us in the same van. My companions and I agreed that we would try and get hold of him as soon as the convoy stopped.

We finally arrived, drenched in sweat in the oppressive heat. I was unable to recognize the place when the soldier unbolted and opened the door of the van, but I heard one of our comrades shout, "Mark this, everyone. We're at the Abu Zaabal Prison Annex."

My need to urinate increased and the pain in my bladder became excruciating when I realized that a grand reception awaited us. The voices of the soldiers and officers here and there were raised so that I made out insults we had almost forgotten in the short period we spent in Hadara Prison. They shouted and screamed,

"Kneel, son of a bitch. Kneel, bastard."

"Crouch down. All of you, squat."

This turned out to be the first stage, which consisted of continuous beatings with sticks, because the second stage started immediately with another feast of more violent beatings intended to make us bend facing the floor, the beatings intensifying on anyone who raised his head.

There were many of them, the blows coming from everywhere. It was impossible to think of anything at all. The important thing was to overcome this first show of violence with which they received us, and to not buckle or drop to the ground. The key thing was to stay alert and keep your arms at the ready to protect your head.

Ibrahim al-Shahawi

The three of us who were sitting close to each other were ordered to run. Each of us was carrying his suitcase. Shuhdi, the tallest among us and who was to the extreme right, seemed like a giant as he strode ahead of us into the raging fire. Yes, it felt as if the mysterious area stretching ahead of us had been set on fire. I observed as closely as I could the groups that had preceded us. Each two were tied together, next to them another pair. Everyone was running between two rows of jailers who would catch us with cudgels and sticks. At the back, there was another officer mounted on a horse with a whip in hand. I was afraid of dropping to the ground because when I managed to steal a glance while we were kneeling, I caught sight of Hasan al-Manawishi who had arrived two groups ahead of us: he had fallen before getting to the end and I saw with my own eyes the horse trampling him while he screamed at the top of his voice. I also managed to make out each group as it was forced to slow down in front of the seated officials, at the center of whom was General Himmat with al-Halawani, surrounded by many high-ranking officers all in uniform, their decorations pinned on their chests.

Shuhdi was the only one who had been untied and allowed to run freely, carrying his suitcase like us, whereas I was tied to Saad al-Sai. The three of us went on running together, with the jailers' blows falling on our bodies, but Shuhdi alone was free. I realized then that they had decided to break his bones at a private welcome ceremony.

After about two hours of squatting, the running was bearable, despite the blows that kept coming from all directions, while the voice of the officer on horseback and the sound of his whip reached us from the rear. When Shuhdi preceded us by a step or two the officer caught up with him and singled him out with his whip, driving him screaming ahead. The blows increased from right and left. The suitcase felt heavy in my hand, almost slipping out of my grip. The handcuff tying me to Saad caused us to fall several times, but we would get up hastily as the belt lashes followed us. When we got close to the high officials, Himmat screeched in his effeminate voice, "That boy, Shuhdi, over there. I want his voice to reach me here."

"What's your name, boy?" the officer on horseback demanded.

Shuhdi answered while the blows were raining down on him, "You know who I am, Abd al-Latif Rushdi. This is a disgraceful way to treat people."

Just then I remembered that criminal Abd al-Latif Rushdi whom I came to know when I was detained in Tora Prison two years ago. He shouted again, "Say 'I'm a bitch,' boy!"

Shuhdi answered promptly, "We are a nationalist movement that supports the president. And even if we didn't, this is barbaric."

Beating him harder, Abd al-Latif Rushdi screamed, "He says he is a nationalist movement, the son of a bitch, sir."

"Drag him, son. Drag him in front of me."

We slowed down in those few minutes when they were occupied with Shuhdi, and were startled to see another group of soldiers chasing him alone. They screened him off from our view. Then the rows of jailers surrounding us snapped to attention and quickly attacked us with their sticks. We started running again while they were dragging Shuhdi within our sight. When he lost consciousness they dunked him in the nearby canal then carried him back to Abd al-Latif Rushdi who quickly tackled him with his whip. But what amazed me was that Shuhdi managed to sustain it and remained standing.

Abd al-Latif yelled, "What's your name, Shuhdi boy?"

"You know, Abd al-Latif Rushdi, you."

"I want to hear you say 'I am Shuhdi the bitch, the bitch.'"

"I am Shuhdi Attiya, Abd al-Latif."

"Say 'I am Shuhdi the bitch.'"

Shuhdi said nothing.

"Well then, I'm waiting for you. Pound him! I want him to get his heart's content today."

We had reached the inner gate of the courtyard past the officials, to be received by another officer with a sergeant and a number of jailers, then the barber too. They forced us to kneel in front of the barber who sheared off our hair, one after the other, at top speed, while the jailers took turns beating us. They also forced us to strip and stand stark naked. I overheard Himmat's voice coming from the rear, "That boy, Shuhdi, marry him off. Since he won't say he's a bitch, put him on the maiden. Marry him off."

His effeminate voice echoed through the almost total silence, broken only by the insults of the officers and jailers as they dragged Shuhdi, who was still wet from having been dipped several times in the nearby canal, then stretched him out on the wooden maiden and went about whipping him.

As for the rest of us, a prison uniform was thrown at each, together with a bowl for prison grub and a tattered blanket. But then I could no longer bear it, could no longer stand anything—at all.

Roxanne

She had no option but to leave her daughter Hanan with her mother in Alexandria and follow from a distance in the trail of the fourth and last van after the convoy had set out shortly before dawn. Fatigue and driving at night had rattled her body, which felt as if it was coming apart. She would have dozed off had it not been for the striking desolation of the desert in the early morning hours at the beginning of the road to Abu Zaabal Prison with which she was familiar from Shuhdi's successive imprisonments. She felt like lighting a cigarette but resisted the temptation as one of the soldiers might catch sight of her and harass her.

Ever since Shuhdi was arrested and transferred to Hadara Prison she had moved from Cairo to Alexandria where she was staying with her father and mother. She devoted all her time to him, following up with the lawyers and braving no end of trouble going back and forth between the prosecutor and State Security to get a permit to visit him, each foisting the responsibility for issuing the permit on the other. She did not see Shuhdi all through the trial except once in the courtroom as he was standing among his companions in the dock. His eyes were shining, she thought, as he sent her kisses in the air. They managed, though, to steal a few minutes in which their hands touched across the iron dock like two teenagers.

Roxanne, a Greek born in Egypt, went against the grain of the upbringing her parents were keen to give her among her peers in the Greek community when she fell in love with the senior inspector of English language in secondary schools who was constantly in and out of prison. From the minute she met him at one of the seminars at the House of Scientific Research, something about his broad shoulders and towering height made her fall head over heels for him. Shuhdi overwhelmed her with his tenderness, enveloping her completely. The daughter they had after two years of marriage was the spitting image of her father, so much so that all Roxanne needed to do to have dreams of Shuhdi was to look at her face before going to bed.

The five years she had so far spent with him were fraught, but he always made it up to her during the spells when he was out of prison. He would make sure they often dined out alone together which, as he knew, made her very happy. His rare gentleness so bound her to him that she craved his approval. It was he who chose to name their daughter Hanan, meaning tenderness. Roxanne and Hanan: he drew them closer into his captivity, folding them both under his wings.

She became adept at organizing protest campaigns and contacting lawyers and the press, her English and French, as well as her Greek of course, being an asset in this respect. But Shuhdi's imprisonment this time was different from any other before. She had taken on the task of going every week to report on the latest to the families, lawyers, and those of his comrades in the movement who were still free, and staying in contact. But this transfer was much more worrying: the circumstances made her expect treachery. Setting out before dawn, she drove after them, keeping at a reasonable distance so as not to lose sight of the last van. She could not bring herself not to go: I'll just find out which prison they're taking him to, and there's no difference really between Abu Zaabal Prison and any other jail, she reasoned.

The sun had now risen and, feeling the sting of thirst, Roxanne stretched. It was another hot day and the humidity made it all the more sweaty and tedious. She felt sticky and wished she could have a warm bath and go to bed after making sure her husband was safe. She stretched again and lowered the window on her side.

The silence of the soldiers guarding the entrance to Abu Zaabal zone, the point beyond which she could not go further, caught her attention. Shortly afterward a motorcade of jeeps overtook her. Then the sound of the bugle echoed from afar and her heart sank at the surprise. Something must be up this sticky, damp morning. She lowered the car window on her side halfway and looked right and left.

The sun was everywhere and the daily noise of cars had started. Seeing that the whole world was up and about gave her courage to light a cigarette. She sat smoking furtively and felt the heavy numbness of the first cigarette. She said to herself she wouldn't leave before finding out what was behind the motorcade of jeeps that had driven past a little while ago. It might be a routine inspection by the Prison Authority; then again it might have been deemed necessary that its officials should be there to deliver this particular group of prisoners. Time went by sluggishly, and feeling weary, she lowered the window halfway again. As long as Hanan was with her grandmother, she had nothing to worry about. The important thing now was to set her mind at ease about Shuhdi then she would go to the lawyers so that everyone would know that the whole case had now been transferred to Abu Zaabal.

It seemed to her she had dozed off for a few minutes. She saw him—Shuhdi. He had misplaced his eyeglasses and stood blinking with his hands outstretched. Still he was laughing as he said, "Hand me my glasses."

This was his habit whenever he woke up. The eyeglasses were right in front of him on the dining room table. She kept trying to raise her voice to caution him that he was about to bump into the table. Someone was shackling her and pressing down on her mouth. She suppressed her gasp when he actually bumped into the table and started to fall slowly to the floor. She finally summoned the strength to get rid of whoever was shackling her and took Shuhdi's head in her arms. Shuhdi was silent but she felt his warm, sticky blood.

She opened her eyes. The hand with which she had held his head to her was still warm; she raised it and gazed at it. Her palm was white and her fingers were slender as always, yet she still felt the stickiness of warm, wet blood almost preventing her from moving her fingers freely. She lit another cigarette with the same furtiveness, then had to move it to the other hand which had not touched Shuhdi's head in her fleeting dream and was less sticky.

She saw them in the distance coming out of the prison gate. They were a number of guards on their way home, it seemed, after their shift was over. She stubbed out the cigarette and hurried out of the car. She was not sure how to act as she went toward them. But then she caught sight of one of them, who seemed so young he looked like a boy. She went up to him, driven by an irresistible force, until she had almost bumped into him. She tried to raise her voice, "What happened? Tell me what happened."

She couldn't tell whether the sight of her scared the boy or whether he was so startled to see her in front of him that he couldn't help blurting out what had terrified him only a moment ago. His shift had ended midday, and he was standing above the quarry with his machine gun pointed at the prisoners ever since they went down. He saw the high officials and the very tall man they'd taken aside and beaten violently until he'd fallen to the ground then was dragged around. Next he saw them hurrying to leave the place in their cars without the bugle marking their departure. He found out later that one of the prisoners called Shuhdi had been beaten to death. To Roxanne, who had picked him out of all the soldiers and jailers, he answered, "Seems a guy called Shuhdi died. Heard them say one of the prisoners called Shuhdi died."

Fortunately for her, the car was nearby. She headed for it before she could drop to the ground. She held up until they had left. Then she burst into a long fit of weeping without the slightest sound escaping her. "I knew it in my heart," she mumbled as her tears fell profusely. She felt her heart shudder as though it was as heavy as a stone. "How could you have allowed them to kill you, Shuhdi? Why did you let them kill you, love? My God! They're a pack of dogs. Murderers, yes, murderers."

6

Alia got addicted to her computer and could no longer do without it. She used it as a word processor for her work, archived her material on it, and kept up e-mail correspondence with many friends, some of whom she'd met by mere chance—and that was apart from all the compact discs she owned. Still, she often got bored with it all. But it had to be said that she always found on the internet topics to propose at the office: beauty queens and movie stars; the weirdest and funniest crimes; this season's makeup; African safaris; the sexiest destinations in South East Asia; women's health tips; how to do flower arrangements and take care of indoor plants; the most reliable methods to conquer boredom, get rid of the smell of sweat, and ensure the happiness of every member of the family. All these topics were so much in demand that she sometimes just went ahead and translated straight from the internet, without clearing things first with the managing editor.

As for Shaker's papers and notes, which petered out in November 1990, they were riddled with gaps, but she managed to fill these in over e-mail with Abd al-Wahab. As things fell into place, she began to suspect that Shaker had become obsessed with the notion that this—an Arab country occupying another—was a spectacle not to be missed, and that it might be a long time before it was repeated. In one of her messages to Abd al-Wahab, Alia admitted that her true father had been her Aunt Iqbal who, until the final crisis that led to her suicide, never lost faith that her brother was still alive. Abd al-Wahab in turn relayed to her his brother Luai's account. What had caught Luai's attention about Shaker was the plump body, dressed in civilian clothes, with no head: had his head been there, as with dozens of corpses that were battered by the raids, he wouldn't have noticed him. She wrote back saying that it seemed to her that her father had been almost deliberately courting death. He could have returned, after all, right after Iraq invaded Kuwait without losing much, and perhaps if he'd done so her aunt's condition wouldn't have deteriorated to the point of committing suicide. Their relationship used to give her aunt a sense of security, especially after they moved in together, when Shaker got his divorce and Iqbal returned from Germany, to which she had fled her generation's predicament and the caving in of so many of them. When Alia explained that Iqbal's posthumously published book had given her insight into the depth of the trauma of her aunt's generation, what gave him pause was her aside about her own generation. They had managed, unconsciously perhaps, she suggested, to get past "all those certitudes of your generation," to be more in sync with the way of the world now and to remain unencumbered by anyone. "You may not know this," he wrote back, "but your aunt's book was photocopied over and over again to be circulated among Arab exiles—intellectuals, leftists, and dissidents—in various European capitals." It was months after the book's publication that he managed to land a photocopy. They all read it as an exoneration of their defeat and the contempt in which they were subsequently held, he added. "We felt she had vindicated us in her book, and it was as if her suicide was the price she paid to redeem us all," Abd al-Wahab wrote, adding that her friends had been smart to publish the book right after Iqbal's death. He asked Alia if she had any unpublished writings by her, and she sent him samples of Iqbal's papers that she had kept after the move to the Hilmiya apartment, which, fortunately, no one had tampered with. Iqbal's book *Cancer of the Soul* had been saved in the computer of the friend who had typeset it, and who had given Iqbal a printout, though by then she was in the early stages of her final illness and had taken no interest in it. It was thanks to this master copy, which her friend had kept, that the text was salvaged and the book was published in its entirety. All that remained with Alia was loose sheets, including a poem she was particularly fond of that she sent to Abd al-Wahab:

Lovers expire
not through passion
but asphyxia,
even the act of love has turned into
an act of murder, blood-sucking,
even the innocent are killed
even the kind;
in an age that denies emotions
the ensuing hollowness fills people with
arrogance and tyranny:
it is then that the executioner's might is
gauged by the size of the head he hurls off—

hence the horizon is
blocked by mounds of skulls.

Abd al-Wahab said he was taken aback by the excessive harshness of the poem, but he did ask for more of Iqbal's texts. Alia sent him an excerpt from Iqbal's journal:

At times my soul is turned inside out by dint of one of those transports of joy afforded you ever-so-rarely in a lifetime, when your emotions become as the certitudes of faith and you are transformed into a mass of happiness all ears and eyes, and you see and discover as you never have before, and everything seems perilous, because in fact your very soul is on the brink in such moments. This is when you vanish. Now in my fifties, I realize that the mistake I persistently, almost methodically, made was precisely those daydreams, or rather my assumption that the instance of grasping the dream was everlasting truth.

Alia sent him other samples of Iqbal's writings. Drawing her attention to the similarities between Iqbal's papers and her father Shaker's, Abd al-Wahab suggested that there was a possible joint book in this material. It would bring together Shaker's papers written in the aftermath of the invasion of Kuwait by Iraq and going up to the first hours of the Allied air raids just when he had made up his mind to return and had boarded the bus that was to be overtaken by the F-16 missiles. As for Iqbal's papers, these would comprise several examples of her poetry, her reflections on tenderness and cruelty, on her leftist friends, and the bygone days of the student movement, as well as the journal she kept during her illness. Alia wrote back that the journal her aunt kept during her illness was her property, and that she had sent it to him just for his private perusal and not for publication. "In any case," Abd al-Wahab replied, "I respect your wishes. I'm thinking we should meet in two months' time, say around the New Year's holidays. Shall we enter the new millennium together? What do you say? I'll be getting ten days off then and can make arrangements to come to Cairo—if, that is, you should be so generous as to accept!"

What they shared suddenly looked like love.

They had exchanged their photos over e-mail in the first months of their correspondence. Alia had probably already fallen in love with him before seeing his photo. It was one of her bouts of recklessness over which she had no control. She realized, of course, that what was going through her head was sheer madness. But it brought to mind one of her aunt's journal entries in which she had written about a novelist she had fallen in love with on reading his first novel, a passion that only grew as she pored over the rest of his books. And when Iqbal laid her snares, to meet him just once, she who never had a knack for this sort of thing finally got her way. But she found nothing but an old man who feared his wife more than he did the government and authority. She could not help bursting out laughing right in his face as she sat opposite him for the first time at a café on the Nile, on the outskirts of the Shubra district, that he picked at her insistence to meet him. She startled him in mid-sentence with her outburst of laughter and, as she hurriedly got up to leave, she threw out that she had forgotten an important appointment.

Alia, who could not remember the novelist's name, wondered if a propensity toward mad passion could be genetically transmitted. Was she destined to reenact, some two decades later, her aunt's misadventure?

Although Abd al-Wahab was twenty-two years her senior, she never once experienced the age difference throughout the dozens of messages they had exchanged. He had written to her that Iqbal had drawn them close to each other, that it was indeed to her that he owed Alia's acquaintance. Alia inwardly agreed: Iqbal had had a hand in her attraction to him, just as she had previously had a hand in her relationship with Fouad al-Shafie, who had one day come up to her to introduce himself, a copy of *Cancer of the Soul* in his hand. Iqbal had been a powerful presence in her life ever since her father Shaker had traveled to Kuwait on the eve of the Iraqi invasion. Her aunt had taken full responsibility for her until she committed suicide by leaping from the terrace of the ninth-floor Hilmiya apartment. After her death, Iqbal continued to exert her presence through her book *Cancer of the Soul* and here was Alia discovering yet new papers of hers, as well as those of her father.

It felt almost like a contemporary scenario by her father. Before she could pluck up the courage to write to Abd al-Wahab about this scenario she had dreamt up and their respective roles in it—he as the Iraqi in his Nordic exile, and she as the Egyptian woman twenty-something years his junior, meeting over e-mail— he had surprised her with the dramatic offer that they spend New Year's Eve together. He also pled with her to accept his suggestion that they co-edit a book comprising Iqbal's and Shaker's papers. Alia couldn't contain her excitement about his New Year's Eve offer and said she would take a few days off from work to devote her time to him. Abd al-Wahab wrote back that he was going to book his ticket immediately; Cairo, he added, was one of the capitals bound to enter the new century with much pomp and ceremony, and indeed the international press was already going on about a gala to take place on the Pyramid Plateau. Alia shot back that she would try and get hold of two tickets via the bureau she worked for, and if that didn't work, she'd just pay the two hundred pounds, come what may.

With difficulty he managed to book a flight two days before the New Year's celebrations and sent her his last e-mail a few hours before landing in Cairo. Alia had advised him to stay at one of the downtown hotels. In the cab from the airport he asked the driver a few questions and settled on the Cosmopolitan Hotel. Even before getting to his room he called Alia from the reception.

"I've been waiting by the phone since I got your message. Where are you now?"

"Downtown, at the Cosmopolitan, just as you suggested."

"Great. I'll meet you at six, at the coffee shop, to give you time to get some rest and get ready for your first evening in Cairo. Bye for now."

At first, he seemed confused, almost perturbed. He said that all through the flight he kept turning over in his mind the sequence of coincidences, that were nevertheless significant when considered all together, which had finally led them to each other. "You are more beautiful than in the photo, of course, and you also resemble Iqbal in the picture on the back cover of *Cancer of the Soul*." Alia felt that the words brought Iqbal back to her, suffusing her with a warm sense of security.

Even though they felt a certain familiarity, they stole diffident glances to ascertain each other's features. The age difference had no effect on her, although the years of exile had etched themselves across his serene dark face and his graying sideburns that she found alluring from the start.

He had brought a few copies of his book on Basra that had been published in Beirut three months earlier. While they were having coffee, he penned a dedication to her: "To the memory of significant coincidences, with utmost gratitude to your person and to the coincidence that led me to you."

"A very nice dedication, Abd al-. . . " She trailed off as she mumbled her thanks.

"It's Abd al-Wahab, dear. The name is Abd al-Wahab, Alia," he quickly prompted her.

They set out from the hotel. As they got out of the cab at the corner of al-Muizz Street, a whiff of al-Ghuriya's aromas, with all its spice and scent shops, caught Alia in the face. Every time she came to this district she was intoxicated by its sharp fragrant blend that wafted in gusts to reach her even on the outskirts of Gammaliya. She remembered that it was to Fouad al-Shafie that she owed her intimate knowledge of the district and passion for it. For over a year, she had spent hours on end just about every day wandering around with him there. She came to know every inch of the area all the way from Bab al-Khalq—which was a stone's throw away from her father's family house, though she was barely aware of it until she met Fouad—to the bus stop right next to Sidi al-Jaafari Mosque in Darrasa.

Of the aroma of al-Ghuriya, Fouad used to say it mellowed your very bones. He taught her to pick it out at a distance as they walked down from Bab Zuwayla. He would lead her as they sauntered through al-Ghuriya's maze of narrow alleyways as if it were a feast for all the senses.

When she managed to get a grip on herself she pulled her black leather jacket tightly around her and gestured toward the wall and dome to their right.

"Sir, I'll be your guide for the evening," she said. "This here is the Ghuri dome. I expect you've heard about Sultan al-Ghuri?"

"Oh, yes."

"He was the last of the sultans of the Mamluk Dynasty who fought the Ottomans and was defeated by them in the Levant. He is probably the only sultan who was not buried in the mausoleum he built for himself during his reign."

"As I recall, he died beneath the horses' hooves during that last battle."

She drew closer to him. "Actually, my knowledge of history is scanty except for this period, and that on account of my love for this place." He patted her shoulder but she pulled away from him with a bothered look. As he registered her reaction he hastened to match his step, as if apologetically, and pointed to a nearby minaret.

"This is Abul-Dahab Mosque, followed by al-Azhar Mosque, and right behind it is an area called al-Batniya where hashish used to be sold quite openly."

They walked through the dirty underpass amid the beggars who dotted the passage and thronged the entrance. She leaned ever so slightly toward him as they climbed up the last steps heading for the square, as if making up for her brusqueness. It was chilly, now that night had fallen, and Abd al-Wahab, wrapped in a dark woolen coat, looked willowy as he stepped aside every now and then to let Alia lead the way. The alleyways and the houses, he remarked, reminded him of old Basra. "Anyway, I've never been so lucky as to be accompanied by such a beautiful young woman, and so knowledgeable about one of the most renowned and mysterious cities in the world."

She took him in the direction of Khan al-Khalili. Once past the Husayn Hotel passageway and into the Khan proper, Abd al-Wahab surrendered himself to the experience. The alleyways were almost empty, the chill in the air dictating the pedestrians' slow, deliberate pace. He peered through the store windows, drinking in all they held—prayer beads; scarabs; wood carvings; silver- and copper-work; kohl sticks and jars; Qur'an holders; trays, plates, and waterpipes; statues of gods and pharaohs; divans in the corners and pharaonic- and Mamluk-style chairs; sequined fabrics; chunks of stone; perfumes; mummified animals, tigers, and hawks; the ankh, key of life; pendant lamps; ornaments and gold jewelry. There were stores, side by side to the right and to the left, the passageways between them just wide enough for two people. He barely paused now; try as he might, he was too enchanted to stop. Alia was observing him closely with a hint of a smile on her face. She felt comfortable with Abd al-Wahab, indeed, almost drawn to him. Something about his face, gestures, and sentences that ended as suddenly as they began suggested restraint. He had a manly timidity that Alia liked and that set her at ease to act spontaneously. He moved as if mesmerized between the glass panes and mirrors that refracted the light of hidden lamps until they had finally wound their way back to al-Muizz Street.

Alia was not sure why the memory of Fouad al-Shafie came back to her so insistently just then. Things were different with Fouad, the way we discovered each other, she thought to herself. When we read *Cancer of the Soul* together, I could see why my aunt was loved by everyone, especially by her generation, because she had defended it despite its major sins and successive failures that had overtaken its very dreams. Fouad used to say that what amazed him about Iqbal and her generation was their ability to dream, they who had left everything in ruins for their successors. He's right, Alia thought, I have no dreams, no wishes whatsoever. At most I may have dreamt that my mother and I would be able to beat her cancer, and that Fouad and I should stay friends despite our failure to love each other. She had to admit that she owed Fouad not only her passion for Gammaliya but also her good times with his wacky friends whom she used to meet whenever he took her to the Hurriya Café for a glass of beer or to the Bustan Café where they would sit in the wide passageway that had witnessed so many violent fights between the touts who service tourists over their sleazy customers.

Sensing Abd al-Wahab's eyes on her, she gestured toward a narrow alleyway opposite.

"See this alley here? It's called Alley of the Jews. They used to live there until the 1956 Suez War."

"We too have an Alley of the Jews in Basra. I think they even had a whole quarter to themselves in Baghdad."

"There are hardly any Jews still living here of course. I remember reading a feature article that said there were thirty-three elderly women left who have decided to meet their death here where they were born."

"My dear, don't involve me in talk about the Jews or I'll be charged with anti-Semitism!" he said with a smile. "Well, this Khan is a strange, fascinating place. You have such great artists. Only now does it make sense to me that people call Cairo 'Mother of the World.' Would you believe that I feel familiar with Cairo? I have this strange feeling that I've roamed through its alleyways before."

As he walked alongside her in al-Muizz Street, Alia was thinking that they did not really know each other as she had imagined, despite the dozens of messages they had exchanged over a period of three months. His panic at a mere passing reference to Jews did not seem justified to her. She was aware, of course, that Israel waves the specter of anti-Semitism in face of all and sundry. Still, it was odd that Abd al-Wahab, too, should be susceptible to it.

It was probably past nine in the evening by then and the weather was getting chillier. She drew her jacket tightly around her. There were few pedestrians but the cafés here and there were crowded. When they reached the Mosque of al-Salih Najm al-Din Ayyub she paused.

"See the ruins of that mosque there? Its style is different from all the others in this area because it was built in the Ayyubid Dynasty. It's called the Mosque of al-Salih Najm al-Din Ayyub after one of the Ayyubid sultans who ruled Egypt after the Fatimid Dynasty."

In the quiet of the night Abd al-Wahab contemplated the mosque. Its architectural style did seem unique. The façade closest to them, which was floodlit, supported what looked like the vestiges of a tower.

"You're quite right," he turned to her, "though I still think that the biggest surprise is you."

"As I said, this is the one part I know of Egypt, or of the whole world, for that matter. My father had a passion for history, as you know, and it seems I inherited this from him."

"Yes, of course. Anyone who reads the magnificent scenario he wrote about Urabi cannot fail to notice. By the way, we still haven't spoken of the co-authored book by the late Iqbal and Shaker."

"We'll get around to it," she said as she led him across the street. "But first, I want to show you this hammam. It's a popular public bath that was still functioning until a few months ago. And just past it is the finest and most important collection of monuments that was built by Sultan al-Nasir Muhammad ibn Qalawun."

The floodlights gave the minarets and domes a singular presence. He stood gazing raptly and listening to her.

"This is the oldest intact collection of monuments. Had it not been for conservation work we would have lost an invaluable treasure. You really ought to see it all in broad daylight. Only then will you discover the enchantment of the Qalawun collection— the architectural design and the scrupulously calculated alignment of the domes, columns, minarets, entrances, and doorways."

"But the night brings its own enchantment, too."

"See that sabil water-house across the way? It dates back to the Ottoman period. So the street you're walking in is several centuries old."

"What's the name of this street?"

"It's al-Muizz li-Din Allah al-Fatimi Street."

"A single street that bears on either side all these centuries and kings and sultans!"

"Well then, let's keep going. If we walk straight ahead, we'll be crossing into the Ottoman period, heading for Bab al-Nasr gate, the southernmost perimeter of the old city."

"Alia, dear," he broke in, "aren't you too young to be steeped in all these details?"

"As I was saying, I inherited my father's passion for history. Besides, I have a friend who's besotted with this place. He was the one who opened my eyes to Islamic Cairo. Come this way, I have a surprise in store for you."

They crossed the street, and a few steps down the road he stopped again.

"This is incredible! It's nothing less than a theater," he exclaimed.

For the first time she noticed that it did indeed resemble a theater. There were steps leading up to a slightly elevated expanse beneath the arches and semi-arches of hewn stone.

"You have a point, Abd al-Wahab. I hadn't noticed that it looked like a theater. It's called Bayt al-Qadi, the Judge's House. The judge used to sit inside and adjudicate between the people who gather out here in what you've called the theater, waiting for their turn to go in. But this isn't the surprise I had in store for you."

"What could be a bigger surprise than this theater?"

"Follow me."

He followed her across the street where she pointed to a one-story building in front of them.

"This is the police station that Naguib Mahfouz described in his *Cairo Trilogy*."

"Now that is a surprise."

"I assume you've read his *Trilogy*," she said, pointing to the opposite side of the street. "You can imagine that this is more or less the location of the protagonist al-Sayyid Ahmad Abd al-Gawad's house, where his wife Amina would stand behind the latticed window screen every night waiting for him to return."

"Amazing. What can I say?"

"And right here where you see this residential building, there was another house that fell into ruins. This is where Naguib Mahfouz was born."

"This is too much for me at one go."

"Then let's sit at this café."

The café overlooked a small square. She picked two chairs on the pavement. Noticing her wrap her black leather jacket around her, Abd al-Wahab said, "It's bitterly cold. Shall we move inside?"

"It's probably best to stay here so we don't catch cold—it's really warm inside the café. Well, what do you think?"

She watched him smilingly as he knit his eyebrows.

"It's incredible. Truly amazing, Alia. It's nothing less than a stage. All it takes is some chairs you'd spread out here in the square, and then you'd have an audience."

A lean, elderly waiter came up to them with a smile.

"How about some tea with mint? You won't find the like of it anywhere else in the world," Alia offered then turned to the waiter. "Tea with mint, and make it special for the guest."

As the waiter walked away, Abd al-Wahab said, "Alia, give me a minute to get a grip on myself. I came prepared with so much I wanted to say about the co-authored book by Iqbal and

Shaker, but it's gone straight out of my head. I'm feeling quite blank right now."

"We still have some time. How many days will you be spending in Cairo?"

"Ten days. It's all I could get off from work."

"Do you fear the Jews?"

Alia's question caught him off guard and he stuttered as he cast around for an answer.

"Why do you ask, my dear?"

"A little while ago you asked me not to involve you in any talk about the Jews so that you wouldn't be accused of anti-Semitism in Europe."

"I was joking, of course," he broke in. "But it needs to be said that the Jews have a strong presence in Europe and wield much more influence than you'd think. Still, the way I see it, our problem is with Israel and not with the Jews of Europe."

The waiter had brought a tray with a kettle, two glasses adorned with mint sprigs and a sugar bowl. Looking him straight in the eye with a smile, she interrupted to ask how many spoons of sugar he took.

"One spoon. In case you find my stance on Israel confusing, I should explain that I am against it not only because of what it has done to the Palestinians but because of its racism and the religious basis on which it was founded."

"I'm sorry, I didn't mean it," she broke in again. "Palestine and all that's happened to it are close to my heart. I had to boycott Gammaliya in its entirety, much as I adore it, because I kept bumping into Israelis wandering around all over the streets and in the stores. I tell you I was terrified—just watching their hustle and bustle and intrepid sallying down the narrowest alleys it crossed my mind that they were plotting to take over Historic Cairo!" She leaned toward him laughingly.

"The cardinal problem that your late aunt Iqbal's generation confronted was the implanting of Israel in the Arab body and the ceaseless blows it administered to the Arabs."

"My aunt was like a mother and a father—she was everything to me. Whenever I remember her or someone mentions her I feel serene and at peace with myself."

"I can well understand this, as I said over e-mail. If we get to publish a book combining her journal notes and Shaker's we will have kept both their memories alive. Her entire generation owes her a huge debt of gratitude. She was the noblest of them all, and the most courageous and sensitive too."

Alia's eyes filled with tears and she gave a little sob as she whispered, "But for me, she was my entire family. Do you know what it's like to lose your family?"

She stopped in her tracks and could not help bursting out laughing.

"Oh well, I guess no one knows what it's like more than you, Abd al-. . . "

"The name's Abd al-Wahab, dear. You're not going to turn all shy again?"

"Okay, Abd al-Wahab. What was I saying? Oh yes, you more than anyone else would know what it's like to lose your family. Anyway, we need to leave now. Listen, to celebrate your arrival I'll invite you to dinner, just for tonight."

He beamed at her, his eyes embracing her.

"Just for tonight?"

"The thing is that I cashed my salary today. Afterward, the money just flies out of my purse and I can't catch it!"

She threw up her arms in a gesture that gave her a slender, lithe air, her black eyes glistening in the dim light as she stood framed against the theater that had so enchanted him. He stretched out his hand to caress her face but changed his mind halfway and touched her shoulder gently instead.

"You're the most beautiful significant coincidence, Alia."

In all the messages she had sent him she did not once make the slightest reference to any relationship; in fact, she often complained of loneliness. The age difference that had made him restrain himself whenever he wrote to her no longer seemed such a big issue, though he still strained to pick up a signal from her. He had never imagined that all this would happen to him with an Egyptian girl, such a beautiful one at that, so delicate and, to top it all, unattached.

He let Alia lead the way and followed down into what looked like a vault with a low ceiling. They turned left into a cobbled winding alley and he caught up with her.

"You know, I'm still apprehensive about showing my mother the envelope with my father's papers," she said casually.

"I feel for you. You'll probably have to wait until she's fully recovered."

"I think I said this in one of my e-mails, but it's not just my mother who won't be able to bear it. I don't think I can deal with it either. Do you have any idea what it's like to know that your father's head is lost? Your brother Luai, as you yourself told me, found my father headless. Where is his head? In Kuwait or in Iraq?"

"I don't think it makes a difference. His head would be buried in any case, in whichever country it was found in." After a short pause, he continued, "What do you say about writing the introduction to the co-authored book we'll be editing together? After much thought, this is what I feel would be best, and I'd been planning to suggest it when we met."

They had taken another turn and she pointed to a small yellow building nearby.

"This is the government mint. You know what that is, don't you?"

"Yes, just as I can read and write!"

As they burst out laughing their shoulders touched and they remained close as they trod the stones of the alley in semi-darkness.

"Listen. We're quite close to the shrine of Umm al-Ghulam, 'The Boy's Mother.' Hers is quite a story. Ready to hear it?"

"Yes, dear."

"It's a very beautiful story. Umm al-Ghulam, a kind Egyptian woman, was sitting at home when into her lap landed the head of al-Husayn, which, after his murder at Karbala, had fled to Cairo, with the caliph's soldiers in pursuit. According to the biographical narrative about Umm al-Ghulam, she slew her son and threw his head to the caliph's soldiers to save al-Husayn's head, which is buried here. Umm al-Ghulam's shrine still exists and to this minute it exudes the scent of musk and amber, yes, to this very minute. I can take you to her shrine right now and you'll be able to smell it for yourself. There's only one little problem—a historical problem that the account overlooked, namely that Cairo hadn't been built yet when al-Husayn was murdered."

Alia was breathless as she narrated the story. She fell silent as the lights from the widening street reached them while they slowly approached the al-Husayn Mosque.

Part Three

AL-HUSAYN'S MURDERERS WERE NOT *the only ones with such black hearts. Impalement and dismemberment were devised by the Assyrians and further developed by the Ottomans. As for burning at the stake, this was practiced in Europe before Joan of Arc; the number of men burned by the Inquisition in a single year came to two thousand, and it was also in the course of a single year that Calvin put to death fourteen women whom the church council in Geneva had accused of conjuring up the devil and conspiring to lure him to the city. Dózsa, the leader of the 1541 peasant uprising in Hungary, was captured by the princes who roasted him by having him sit on a burning hot chair, before they gave his fellow captives the choice between eating his roasted flesh or being roasted in the same manner—and of course some of them accepted and ate him. Rohrbach, a rebel in the German countryside who was a contemporary of Dózsa's, was tied to a pole and surrounded by low flames until he had been roasted to death. The museum of the Institute of Ethnicities in Beijing still includes among its exhibits samples of flayed human flesh; the flaying of serfs continued to be the standard procedure of disciplining them in Tibet until 1951. In the Middle Ages, the feudal lords of central Europe invented quartering and skewering with red hot metal rods. This is not to mention what the Spanish conquistadors committed in the New World: in a very few years they had exterminated seventy million Indians. Indeed, when a soldier's dog barked from hunger, the man looked around him and, spotting an Indian woman breastfeeding a child, he snatched the child from its mother's breast and threw it to the dog. So consider yourself lucky, he said to himself, forced as he was to gaze at the sun, his head being stuck to the iron bridge, reminiscing about what had happened to him in the past.*

1

l-Husayn spent his last night in Karbala. His son Ali was ill, and was being nursed by his aunt Zaynab who held him in her arms. He heard his father and realized that a calamity had befallen them when his aunt leapt up screaming, "Would that death had deprived me of life! They have all died—Fatima, Ali, my father, and Hasan, my brother—and I have no one left but you."

Running his eyes across a sky illuminated by thousands of small sparkling stars, al-Husayn turned to gaze at her tenderly. "Little sister, let not the devil rob you of your composure."

"You are as my father and my mother, O father of Abdullah. I would lay down my life for you," she promptly answered.

Slapping her face and rending her clothes, she fell unconscious. Al-Husayn poured some water on her face, murmuring, "Sister, have fear of God, for all things are destined to perish but His face."

The following day, al-Husayn mobilized his companions, of whom there were thirty-two horsemen and forty footmen. His brother al-Abbas ibn Ali received his banner. They turned their backs on their tents and al-Husayn gave orders that the kindling and cane left behind be brought and set on fire. The sound of hooves coming from the direction of Ibn Ziyad's encampment reached them from afar. Soon they made out the horseman and the sound grew clear as he drew nearer.

"Husayn," he said, "you hastened to bring hell's fire on yourself before the Day of Resurrection!"

Al-Husayn asked his companions standing around him, "Is that Shamir ibn Dhi al-Jawshan?" When they confirmed it, he said, "Son of a goatherd's woman, it is you who will roast in it."

One of his companions went up to al-Husayn. "Shall I shoot the wretch with an arrow?"

"Do not shoot him. I am loath to be the one who starts it."

When Shamir turned back it seemed that the outcome of the battle had already been settled. But no sooner was he out of sight than another horseman racing the wind appeared then stopped in front of al-Husayn. It was al-Hurr ibn Yazid.

"Do you remember me?" he mumbled breathlessly. "I am the companion who prevented you from going back, who accompanied you on the way, had you halt in this spot, and asked you to pledge allegiance to Yazid. Do you not remember me? I am al-Hurr ibn Yazid, and I have come to you in repentance to die between your hands."

Al-Husayn's eyes welled up with tears, and cheerfulness spread among his companions, for it was of no small import that Ubaydallah ibn Ziyad's commander should join their ranks.

Opposite al-Husayn more than five thousand men lay in wait, while he and his companions were seventy-three men. They and their horses were wracked with thirst, as were the women who, together with their children, were crouching in the tents following al-Husayn's instructions.

On every side they surrounded and besieged him. They barred him from moving freely in God's lands to reach safety with his people and companions, just as they barred him from the waters of the Euphrates from which Jew, Magi, and Christian drink and in which, indeed, even the pigs and dogs of the Sawad wallow.

Umar ibn Saad shot the first arrow, but the soldiers balked and soon the horses bolted and threw over their riders. Thereupon Shamir gave orders to have the nearest soldier slain so fear spread among the rest and they returned to their positions. Then Yasar, a client of Ziyad ibn Abi Sufyan's, along with a client of Ubaydallah ibn Ziyad's, sallied forth and called for opponents to come out to them. So it went at first.

Two of al-Husayn's companions would ask permission to fight and would attack two horsemen from the usurper's army and finish them off. His companions fought valiantly to their utmost ability. None of them was martyred before killing four or five of the usurpers. Shamir settled the matter by charging with his soldiers. When al-Husayn's companions stood firm, the unrighteous had someone set fire to the camps sheltering the women and children. Just then, al-Kalbi's wife saw her husband drop from his horse and ran out to sit at his head and wipe the dust off him.

"Felicitations on attaining paradise," she said.

Shamir turned to his boy-servant Rustum and ordered him, "Strike her head with the pole."

The boy smashed the woman's head and she died on the spot. Meanwhile, Shamir launched forth until he had struck al-Husayn's tent with his spear, then called out, "Bring me fire that I may burn down this abode on top of its inhabitants."

All this took place after al-Hurr ibn Yazid had been killed. It was then that al-Husayn's companions realized that the final moment was nigh, for here they were unable to protect either their friend or themselves. They rushed to meet their death by his side.

The first of al-Husayn's people to be killed was his son, Ali. Murra ibn Munqidh blocked his way and stabbed him, then the unrighteous encircled and hacked him with their swords. A woman like the rising sun came out from the campsite, crying, "O my brother! O my nephew!"

This was Zaynab, the daughter of Fatima, who took the noble body into her arms. But al-Husayn drew her by the hand back to the tent. Going back to his son, he gestured to those standing around, "Carry your brother."

A boy whose face was as a sliver of the moon, clad in a shirt and tunic, the strap of one of his sandals broken, came out with a sword in his hand. He struck a man with his sword, then another, only to receive a sword's blow on the head from a third. Falling face down, he screamed, "O my uncle!"

Al-Husayn sprung up out of nowhere to strike the head of the man who had struck his nephew. Getting off his steed, he took his brother al-Qasim into his arms and pressed him to his chest. Just then, a man from the Kinda tribe, Malik ibn al-Nusayr, stepped forward and dealt al-Husayn a sword's blow on his burnoose at the head. The burnoose tore and the sword lacerated his head so the garment filled with blood. Al-Husayn called for a cowl that he put on as he cast off the burnoose which his attacker took as booty. Another boy from al-Husayn's people emerged holding a stick he had fetched from behind the camp-site. He was frightened, and as he turned to look right and left the two pearls in his earlobes bounced. A soldier swiftly attacked him, bending down as far as he could on his horse to sever the boy's head. At a loss for what to do, al-Husayn stopped in his tracks, for here were his people and his companions dropping all around him. A boy who was his relative came toward him, and when his sister Zaynab rushed to him, al-Husayn urged her, "Keep him in."

The boy eluded her and hurried toward al-Husayn. He had almost reached him when Bahr ibn Kaab bore down on al-Husayn with his sword. Catching sight of the man, the boy trembled and screamed, "What, killing my uncle, you son of a vixen?"

The blow he received on his hand hacked it all but for the skin. Seeing his hand dangling, he cried, "O Mother!"

His uncle hugged him and shuddered.

From every side they charged on al-Husayn. Zura ibn Sharik struck his left palm then again smote him on the shoulder before retreating in fear. As for al-Husayn, he was resisting and stumbling. Sinan ibn Anas attacked him with a lance and he fell, but when he sought to sever al-Husayn's head he lost his nerve and trembled. The others went about encircling and trying to slay him but also lost their nerve and trembled. Finally, summoning all his courage, Sinan severed the noble head.

His body had sustained thirty-three spear wounds and thirty-four sword blows by then. Sinan hastened to snatch the head, with which he adorned his horse. All that was on the noble body was plundered. His trousers were taken by Bahr ibn Kaab, his cloak made of silk was stolen by Qays ibn al-Ashaath, his sandals were carried off by al-Aswad from the Banu Awd, while his sword was won by a man from the Banu Nahshal. Some of the unrighteous went plundering the turmeric, garments, and camels while others pounced on his belongings, baggage, and even his womenfolk. Though the women struggled to keep their dresses on them, they were crushed and stripped.

Passing as a captive beside her murdered brother, Zaynab, daughter of Fatima, daughter of the Prophet, screamed,

"O Muhammad! O Muhammad! Behold al-Husayn in this bare land, besmeared with blood, his limbs mutilated. Muhammad, your daughters are enslaved, your offspring murdered!"

The tribes proceeded, their horses adorned with the noble heads of al-Husayn's people and his companions. Kinda carried thirteen heads, Hawazin twenty, Tamim seventeen, Banu Asad six, Madhhij seven, and the rest of the army seven.

On the road to Damascus, the seat of the Ummayad court, as the booty was on its way to Yazid ibn Muawiya, al-Husayn's head fled to Egypt, which in the past had given sanctuary to many of the Prophet's descendants. Yazid's soldiers scrambled on its trail, trying to catch up with it. Close to al-Utuf in Cairo, a woman sitting at the door of her house chatting with her neighbor was startled when the noble head came to rest in her lap, exuding the scent of sandalwood and musk, of rosewood and essence of jasmine.

2

THE HEAD SAID to itself:

lived through an afternoon just like this the day I left Ibrahim al-Ghul's café on my way home. At first, I dragged my feet, trying to fix them on the ground. In a little while, though, I experienced this sense of bliss I'd come to expect whenever I was spaced out and could no longer get my bearings. I dashed down the intersecting alleys and roads covered in sweat. It seemed I'd put on weight, and had it not been for the pinch of raw opium I wouldn't have been able to keep on walking with such steady gait. Suddenly finding Faysal Street right in front of me, I hailed a cab. Like the proverbial Abu Zayd, I'm never short of ways and means, I thought to myself.

Only now can I really say I'm back in Egypt, to be precise on Faysal Street headed for Nagat and the children. She'll have barely set the table by now. I'm so hungry I could eat a wolf — then have Nagat for dessert. But this Muhammad Saad I can no

119

longer trust; it looks like he's doing something fishy behind my back. And what kind of an answer was that he threw in my face when I had a word with him about his neglect of the Lada? The son of a bitch. He was a good-for-nothing I picked off the street. And he gets a hundred pounds a month from Nagat, apart from the money he pockets under the table.

Where did all this perspiration come from? Everything grew foggy, then I quickly figured out it was because my eyeglasses were steaming with sweat, so I took them off to wipe the lenses on my shirt but the sleeve was wet too. Was I back in the inferno of the Gulf?

It did seem as if I was back there: even the street was called Faysal. And when did all these stores, in so many sizes and shapes and colors, sprout up? There were supermarkets and stores for anything you can think of: Wimpy's burgers; Light of Islam Electric Appliances; Isra Miracle for Construction Materials; Birioni Sister's Hijab; Prophetic Guidance for Trade and Real Estate; Divine Oneness and Illumination Sportswear Center; Light of Islam Bookstore; Jihad Mini Market; Righteousness Furniture. In the midst of this carnival I'd make my scoop with an entire mall called Hidaya Right Guidance Mall that would sell all sorts of products and goods, with a special focus on readymade garments to capitalize on my experience and knack for landing international brands.

It's only been three years I was away, I thought as I gazed out of the window, and yet I'd returned to find the whole world thronged into this street that had only been a filled-up canal when I last saw it years ago the day I came to buy the apartment. I'd transferred the price of an apartment in a building that consisted of nothing more than the foundations and some columns overlooking the newly drained canal. I still remembered how terrified I was buying thin air, but everyone else at the time was doing it, which emboldened me a little. It wasn't easy to risk such a sum, and though this one financial gamble in my life was ultimately a success, it didn't encourage me to undertake more adventures of the kind that wracks your nerves for years until you've reached terra firma. I even refused Nagat's insistent request to send her power of attorney so she could receive the apartment. I preferred to wait until I got the opportunity to return and receive the apartment myself, which is what I did with the Alexandria apartment too. I always made sure to keep the reins, all of them, in my hands. To the ever-silent Nagat I explained that I did trust her, of course, and that all there was to it was that I needed to keep control of everything so that I could move fast if necessary, and one never knew what might happen. Nagat seemed unconvinced, and yet she remained silent and even-tempered, giving away nothing. Even in the first years of our marriage she never got worked up. It had to be said that she always performed her duties quietly, skillfully, and with the least possible fuss. Then again, this was only after I walloped her repeatedly in our first years together. Because I was sure she really had no close kin, I escalated things a bit so that she'd mend her ways and adapt to my nature as an Upper Egyptian man who would brook no argument. Since then, I didn't recall her having raised her voice except when I was back on my first vacation and asked her to resign from her job and devote herself to the children now that we no longer needed her salary. She refused stubbornly, so I locked the bedroom door and belted her furiously, and though her body swelled I kept at it until she fainted. Then I took off to spend three days on my own in Alexandria.

The taxi was drawing up to our building and I signaled to the driver to stop. I paid him and got out to find the Lada parked at the street corner. Taher, the owner of the kebab restaurant on the ground floor of our building, caught sight of me and came out waving.

"Thank God for your safe return, Hajj. Come in for a second."

At the sound of his voice Mukhtar, the owner of the accessories store, also stepped out. He took hold of my hand and blurted out, "Excuse us, Hajj, there's a matter we need to talk about urgently. Please join us for five minutes."

I had no time for chats about inconsequential matters. No doubt they both wanted to swindle me out of some money. I managed to shake them off before the effect of the hash evaporated and ran up the stairs. I brought out the key to the apartment that I kept with me even in the Gulf and tried to unlock the door but it was no use. It must have been bolted on the inside. When Nagat opened up, I stole a quick kiss but she slipped away from me nervously. I murmured the sweet nothings she loved to hear when we were alone. "Come here, mother of my son. I missed you, girl."

I realized too late that we weren't alone, and straightened up as I walked into the living room. Muhammad Saad was sitting in an armchair in front of the television and Heba was in the armchair beside him. They were watching the afternoon film, which I recognized the minute I saw Suad Hosni in the arms of Ahmad Mazhar. Oh yes, it was *Cairo '30*—as soon as the husband learns that his wife's lover is on his way, he clears out of the house to leave the coast clear for them.

I went back to Nagat and motioned with my head that she should join me in the far hallway.

"Why's he sitting in there, that awful Muhammad?"

"It's nothing, dear. He brought up the suitcases and sat down to catch his breath and wait for your arrival. Now go in and take a shower so we can have lunch."

I left her and went into the bedroom.

Trust Nagat to always make sure our bed was nicely made. The sheets and pillowcases were brand new. The set was pink edged with white lace. The whole room radiated beauty and cleanliness and the scent of her Prophecy perfume. She had pushed the shutters open ever so slightly to let an air current into the room exactly as I taught her when we moved in. I threw my small briefcase on the dresser and emptied out my pockets. Then I went and crouched on the bed.

Fatigue suddenly descended on me as I heard my bones cracking. I went on stuffing my cigarettes using the fastest method I'd come up with so far. I took the tube of my French ballpoint pen and slowly stuck it into the cigarette to make a groove. Then I bit off a piece of hash and stretched it between my fingers until it was the same length as the cigarette. The process engrossed me completely: the hash was so malleable and yielding it drove you to stuff more cigarettes. I pulled out the tube from the cigarette, picked up the pin-like hash and pushed it into the cavity. A whole production line, I thought with a smile. I remembered the bottle of Chivas Regal—that brand really is the essence of whisky. Should I postpone my first glass until the evening? No harm in just one glass before the shower; or maybe I should have another cigarette then decide.

The smoke gathered beneath the ceiling of the room. This was the best hash in the world; its aroma alone was enough to get you high. But where was the photo of Nagat and me? I hung up our wedding picture myself above the dresser on my last trip. The two pictures of Heba and Ali I put inside their frames and propped up on the chest of drawers.

Then I remembered I'd left Muhammad sitting with Heba in the living room. Did I throw him out and shout at Heba to get away from him? I should've shouted at him not her. But did I shout at her? Instead of all this, why shouldn't I just get up and check for myself? I was so hungry for everything—hash, opium, Chivas Regal, stuffed pigeons, rolled vine leaves, a cold shower, reassurance about Ali. But my body took leave of me against my will. This really was the very best hash in the world. You sensed your head had drifted away from you and that you could stretch out your hand and wave to it as it floated around in the room amid the smoke.

I pulled myself together and stretched out my body. When I stood up, I felt giddy and had to shut my eyes until I'd gotten a grip on my body and started directing it at leisure. I found my way to the bathroom and pulled the door behind me. When I'd undressed and was standing naked in front of the mirror, I noticed that my eyes were bloodshot.

Lucky guy, I thought: you deserve all this and much more after ten whole years of hard labor. I stepped into the bathtub and turned on the shower tap, letting the water cascade over me while I gave myself over to the silence with my eyes shut. At first, my perspiration doubled but when I'd adjusted the water temperature to cool my head started clearing and came back to me. I scrubbed my body carefully with the loofah, then washed my hair with the shampoo Nagat had left for me.

I tried to regain my balance but it was no use. What I needed was another sliver of opium to make me feel like a sultan. I heard the doorknob turn and Nagat slipped in.

"May the shower bring you health, bridegroom," she whispered.

She was in a light, sleeveless nightgown, all white and decorated with small flowers, in white too, that barely reached her knees. Holding my underwear in her hands, she closed the door and said, "Muhammad's buzzed off and Heba's gone to her room."

She snatched a towel off the rack and came toward me in measured steps, then started to dry me slowly. I took her in my arms and found her body a bit warm as usual. We got carried away by our first kiss, which was long and drawn out. She sensed my erection and kneaded my penis in her palm with the skill I had so missed. I gasped with pain as she pulled her lips away. As she retreated, she rubbed off the lipstick and murmured, "Put on your underwear. I'll just have to manage. I'll reheat the food."

As she pulled the door shut, I had to face the problem of putting on my underpants in this helplessly erect condition. I'd immersed myself in porno videos and wanking without a thought for the day I'd return to Nagat's arms. I stepped out into the hallway in undershirt and underpants and went into the bedroom. I brought out of the handbag the crimson velvet box that held the *collier* and the bottle of Chivas Regal.

"Nagat, Nagat," I called out.

I had opened the box by the time she returned. The snake studded with diamonds gleamed, and when her eyes fell on it she almost screamed. She picked it up with her fingers and mumbled something. I caught the last words, "Such good taste you have."

She came back to kiss me and I drew my lips away to trace with them one of her nipples. Moaning, she said, "Let's have lunch first. Heba will be eating with us."

She hurried off in a way I found disquieting. Before she'd gone out of my sight I called out, "Bring me a glass with some ice cubes, Nagat. I'll have a quick drink before lunch."

I pulled the bottle out of its case, then pulled hard to uncork it.

I lit another cigarette and sat on the edge of the bed with my torso leaning back and the bottle in my right hand. Nagat came back with a big glass half full of ice cubes. I propped myself up while she sat in my lap and stretched out her hand with the glass. As I took it I leaned over to kiss her this time on her belly. She leaned back against me to allow my face to roam over her belly and vagina. This, too, was one of the secret games no one apart from us knew. Take another example of our codes: that silent

Nagat would not be wearing panties could only mean that she wanted me, right now, and that she was fed up with waiting. But then she drew away and left the room.

I wasn't sure why I felt uneasy again about her tearing herself away from me and her sudden exit. But I downed the drink in one gulp and stubbed out the cigarette. Then I put on a large, short-sleeved galabiya, clean and ironed, that Nagat had laid out for me—or maybe I'd brought it out of one of the suitcases. Let me have another sliver of opium before lunch. Now, how about another cigarette with the second drink, as planned?

With the glass in my hand, I looked at the dresser mirror in front of me. It appalled me to see how flabby I'd become. My paunch was so prominent it pushed out the front of the galabiya. I had lost most of my hair, leaving the top of my head completely bald. I didn't recall ever staring at myself in the mirror for so long. I hadn't noticed all the lines and wrinkles brutally etched on my face. I averted my eyes and downed my second drink in one gulp too. I put out the cigarette and stepped out into the hallway, lugging Heba's suitcase. Then I stopped in my tracks: is this Heba's suitcase? I went back to the room. Where is Ali's suitcase? Oh here it is, the brown suitcase; Heba's is blue. My head became agitated again and my limbs took leave of me. The suitcase felt heavy as I progressed slowly until I had made it to Heba's door and stopped. I could barely make her out lying in the far end of the bed. I edged toward her to find her in the fetal position she always adopted in bed ever since childhood. Her two small knees were bare and the features of her body had started to change, acquiring those astonishingly delicate curves that distinguished Nagat's figure. As my eyes glazed over, I tried to raise my voice. "Heba, get up. Let's have lunch together."

Looks like she's asleep. I'll leave the suitcase by the door of the room, just there.

I turned back and shuffled toward the dining room table. Nagat, who was standing behind one of the chairs, remarked, "Heba's fallen asleep, right? She got up early and must be tired. We'll set her food aside."

She gave me a wink that brought back our complicity. I put my hand through the opening of her nightgown and, while kneading her breast, said, "Fetch the bottle and two glasses with ice cubes. Get a move on."

She extricated herself from my hand and I collapsed into the first chair, trying to resist my erection. I snatched the first pigeon from a whole pile in the huge pyrex dish. It was warm and I fell on it savoring Nagat's skill and special touch with spices that I'd be able to pick out even in an eatery. The rice she stuffed the pigeons with, browned with onions and cooked for just the right amount of time, tasted unlike any other in the world. Nagat returned with two glasses, filled up mine and poured out a small drink for herself. Clinking her glass with mine, she said, "To your health! Isn't that what they say in the movies? Sorry, I'm not drinking much because I can't hold it well."

I downed my next drink in one gulp too, and she poured out another one for me. But I turned to the pigeons and went through one after the other with no end to them in sight. Then I moved in on the vine leaves in the other dish. Life felt glorious and I kept on eating and drinking with a pleasure I had lost for years. Her features now a blur, I exclaimed, "Carry me, mother of my son! Carry me, girl!

I got up and, leaning against her, we proceeded to the bathroom. She stood me by the sink and turned on the tap. She soaped her hands above mine then scrubbed my hands with the foam and washed my mouth and chin. Then she rinsed off the soap with cool water and handed me the towel. She turned to the sink to wash her hands while I went back to the bedroom.

Everything felt like such a heavy weight to drag—my body and arms and belly and eyes. I panicked at the thought that I might let down the hash, the raw opium, the essence of whisky, and the stuffed pigeons if I allowed sleep to overcome me. The solution was to have another sliver of opium, which I did, before topping it all off with a loaded cigarette that I smoked lying on my back naked, waiting for Nagat to join me. She finally came in and I vaguely discerned her taking off her nightgown then walking toward me. I stretched out my body with its erection and she eased herself onto me and I gripped her waist as she writhed on top of me then I drew her hard to me by her breasts. And yet, her body was cold. I tried to hang onto her but the coldness of her body only increased and I sensed that I would not be able to hold back much longer.

When I opened my eyes Muhammad was leaning over me. In his hand was a long knife I had bought in the Gulf, part of a set of the very best imported brands and standing beside him, I quickly noticed, was Nagat, in the same short white nightgown. In an instant, it all fell into place with such vividness that I gasped. Could I have been such an idiot and a pimp?

Isn't this Heba I glimpse peering in between Muhammad and Nagat? What's going on? A hundred thousand dollars of my life was spent to be deposited into three trust funds. Why, Nagat? Weren't you moaning astride me only a minute ago? Either way, my slaying in this manner, and with Heba's connivance—I can't believe it. Muhammad's hand draws nearer and he seems to be saying something. But the pain of beheading is horrendous and I seem to be screaming.

3

ANOTHER DAY BEGINS, and with it another story that I busy myself recollecting as soon as the sun rises in the distant east. My one and only chance to escape the trap set for me every day lies in getting hold of the beginning of the thread. Afterward, I become engrossed in recalling days happy and sad.

There was that day I spent watching the demonstrations with Nagi and Umar, until we lost Nagi halfway through the day. When Umar and I were done with our lukewarm Cokes we walked on down the street that was still packed with malcontents, though the demonstrations were few and far between at the end of the day. The pungent smell of tear gas still filled the air, but for once the Central Security forces did not take us by surprise.

We crossed several streets crowded with angry people, until we reached a huge building with soldiers blocking its entrance and lined up in front of the wrought iron railing surrounding it.

I gazed at the façade, then spotted the scattered shards of the glass sign that had been smashed. I managed to piece together the letters to read: Giza Governorate.

Leaving the building behind us, we walked on and saw another demonstration, just when we thought it had all come to a standstill. The demonstrators were carrying a young man who chanted:

They had us down to tattered clothes
and now they take our bread loaves.

They chanted the words back vigorously as they forged ahead unconcerned with anything. Following this group was another, composed of women and their children, just like the ones we'd seen in Sayyida Zaynab earlier in the day.

Police vans with smashed windshields were parked all along the road. In a little while we started to feel calmer. The pale sun was about to set, and people were worn out at the end of this long day where everyone had chanted slogans against the big shots, the crooks, and the traders. We passed in front of a building set in a large garden with a Mercedes parked in the back. I recognized the model of the car, which was brand new, though the stones had ruined it and smashed the windshield. Right behind it, I glimpsed a big sign that read: Auberge des Pyramides.

Umar stopped, then pulled me toward the sloping street to our right. A boy carrying a big armchair on his head was running down the street. As we drew up, I caught sight of silhouettes of women and men rushing off with all sorts of things that came into view as we ran in their direction: chairs and tables and signs and pictures in large frames. Some of them were clasping vessels and big pots and cups, and highball glasses of the kind you see in movies to their chests. We were so astonished we let go of each other's hands. We'd seen nothing but demonstrations the entire day, and had missed out on the looting of the subsidized food cooperatives in Sayyida Zaynab that the malcontents had broken into.

We watched the people yelling and it looked like they'd only just finished their looting. Some people had put down the chairs and were sitting on them in the small street across from us, while those carrying tables had set them down on the ground. Others who were lugging framed landscapes propped these up against the wall of the first building on that street. There were even people carrying billboards with color pictures of men and women whose names were written underneath—"Shams, Vamp of the Movies," "Nora, the Student-dancer," "Mugharrid, Warbler of the Silver Screen," and other stars who played minor, walk-on roles in movies.

Everyone was tipsy and they were all laughing with mouths wide open. Some people were hugging bottles of what looked like liquor, because I saw the bottle with two dogs on the label, one white and one black, and also beer bottles. Others were making off with chairs, tables, armchairs, pots, and even food. They came out clutching big rounds of roumi cheese, chunks of feta cheese, tomatoes, meat slices, and even huge lumps of raw meat and plucked poultry. All this came from the Auberge night-club that I'd so often heard about but never seen before. There were others who'd stopped by the outer wall to open the bottles, take a swig, and start shouting.

We went back to the other group that had camped out on the street corner and were sitting on the chairs in front of the tables on which they'd set the tins of feta cheese, sacks of tomatoes, roumi cheese chunks, and the bottles of liquor they sipped from time to time. Umar and I didn't have chairs to sit on like the others on that side street overlooking the back door of the Auberge. We just stood around watching and expecting someone to invite us to at least taste the liquor, but no one paid any attention to us. They were sloshed and mellow, and weren't looking at anyone else, just eating and drinking and singing and shouting and chatting and calling out to each other. Umar and I were the only ones standing, and empty-handed at that.

Everything happens so suddenly.

We find them in front of us with their swords and bayonets and penknives. There are many of them, and they have big, well-built bodies. They are all dressed in almost identical short-sleeved black shirts with white bowties. It is as if they are flying as they sweep away whatever is in their way—chairs, tables, armchairs, bottles of liquor, and food—cutting down everyone with their weapons. People are screaming as they flee, while the ones who are injured are crying out. I hear someone yelling that these are the thugs of the Auberge. Umar and I make a mad dash with the others, but the men have laid siege to the entire side street. I see the people who have been hit and stabbed lying on the ground or still sitting in the chairs and armchairs, their bodies and clothes covered in blood. There is nothing to it but to flee to the main street, but a sword strikes Umar right in front of me, and I scream: it has caught him on the crown of his head. In the wink of an eye, another man tackles me and I manage to catch a glimpse of the tip of the bayonet right above my head.

4

EVEN AT NIGHT I NO LONGER got any rest. After sunset, the weather would turn chilly, and it might rain or fog would close in. In any case, my head used to freeze, perched as its remnants were on the tip of the iron bridge. As soon as day broke, bringing with it the chirping of birds that afforded me a modicum of pleasure, I would snatch a few sweet moments of slumber when I forgot about everything. Then the sun would begin its daily business, coming at me amid a crowd of flies and forcing me once again to stare ahead.

D
id you finish that story where they lopped your head off the middle of your neck and took it to the maintenance department of the hospital that had been built by the river on the outskirts of the city for the downloading of programs and replacement of damaged segments? Did you ever finish it?

For four days they had left you without a head, bumping into others, clinging to the nurses who dealt you sudden blows, and exchanging disjointed words with your companions in the ward.

Those were the harshest days, when your organs came apart and you were incapable of pulling them together.

They had tied you to the bed after your body crashed into a closed door while you were bounding down a stairway, unable to steer clear of things in the burst of unshakable recklessness that overtook you. When you woke up, they had affixed your head to your body in the main building, then brought you back only for you to discover you were still tied to your bed with splints all over your legs. Your bones were aching around your pelvis and ribs, while one ankle was fractured, as they explained to you. When the nurse had untied you and helped you put on your clothes in preparation for leaving the ward, she informed you that you needed to return to the hospital for a follow-up on your ankle a week after your discharge. You looked at her quizzically and her wide amber eyes lit up with a smile as she explained that you had suddenly started charging through passages and stairways until you bumped into a closed iron door and that they had managed to treat most of the many bruises and fractures you had. You smiled in turn and thanked her, apologizing for the trouble you had caused them. She surprised you with a mild pat on the cheek and a nod.

The ward was empty except for four newcomers lying headless on their beds, exchanging disjointed words as you had done when you got here a week earlier. The words would issue from that temporary aperture in the middle of the larynx and escape without being processed by the muscles of the tongue and the movements of the lips. Every time you watched them after getting your head changed, you would remind yourself that only a little while ago you were in the same boat. You would wonder why voices became so ugly, so inchoate and broken, whistling and gurgling before finally issuing confused and truncated in the absence of the tongue and lips.

In the end you decided to go out on the wide terrace surrounding all the wards on the floor that overlooked the garden. There they were, too, hanging around without heads and bumping into you while you tried to sidestep them. Nor could you sit because they occupied all the chairs. You leaned against the iron railing but the smell wafting in from the fruit trees by the main building, mixed as it was with the stinky odor of skin and hair, was unbearable, so you retraced your steps to the ward. Then another nurse came and accompanied you outside.

On the ground floor she handed you over to the reception. There the security man informed you that you could have lunch at the cafeteria on the strength of your national identity number and the magnetic ID card while the paperwork for discharging you was being processed.

Ever since you regained consciousness to find your feet and hands tied with cords to your bed and your bones pounded, you had been feeling very ill at ease. You had ascribed your inability to control your limbs to the usual confusion and exhaustion one experiences every time one has a head-change.

After you had lunch, which was flavorless, you tried to exercise your memory; you looked at the magnetic card, but the data recorded on it gave you no clue.

When the security man beckoned to you and handed you your small suitcase, you went in the direction he had pointed and walked out the door. You transferred the suitcase to your right hand and stared at it and turned it over, but it was no help either.

You crossed the remaining stretch of the courtyard, which was hedged with shrubs, and felt the warm sun on your face. When you were past the outer gate a bewitching woman rushed into your arms. Your lips found their way to her cheek and you smelled the scent on her neck. She smelled as fresh and wholesome as a blossom, but you failed to recognize her. She was chattering away, her voice unfamiliar even though, like her, it was enchanting, as was her hair that was light in color, gathered at the forehead, and pulled back in a ponytail. She was well groomed; her black eyes, rimmed with kohl and mascara, sparkled, and her frank, youthful face was dauntless.

She quickly thrust toward you two young girls, as pretty as the moon, who also rushed into your arms as if they knew you. You could easily tell that the girls were the daughters of the bewitching woman whom you had been holding in your arms a minute ago before she stepped back chatting. As for your relationship to the three of them—the woman and her two daughters—you failed to determine it.

When the enchantress, holding you by your right arm, led you to a car parked on the opposite side of the street, while the two girls mischievously clung to your left arm, you realized, just then, as you were approaching the steering wheel not knowing where to start, that there had been some mistake.

5

Abd al-Hamid Haridi

I found myself standing all alone in the observation room after Eid the Blockhead had locked the door and left, while the jailers dumped the other colleagues I had been cleaning and sprinkling the courtyard with into Cell Four. Were they going to forget me in the observation room—the Blockhead and his bosses—amid the sudden pandemonium? Not a single prisoner would dare enter the observation room, and it was not clear when the Blockhead would remember about me.

Shortly thereafter, I heard a commotion and loud voices, so I stood on tiptoe to look through the peephole carved into the door on the inside. I saw the jailers dragging Shuhdi by his legs only four meters away. Yes, it was Shuhdi. I had no trouble recognizing him though he was stark naked and lying face down. Amid the jailers' insults, I could almost make out his low moaning. Just then Abd al-Latif Rushdi came from the rear. If only Shuhdi can withstand the next few minutes, he'll survive, I thought to myself, because the next thing is his hair will be shorn at the barber's, then they'll throw some garments at him and drag him to be thrown into Cell Two which only yesterday had been vacated to receive his group.

None of the cells on either side of the ward allowed any of the inmates to see the passage. Only the observation room, allocated to the jailers, afforded a view of the passage where Shuhdi was stretched out naked in front of me beneath the jailers' feet. His body was swollen with bruises from the blows and he was convulsing every now and then. Although he was the leader of the Democratic Movement for National Liberation, an organization whose political stance supporting Nasser was the opposite of the one I belonged to, Shuhdi in particular had a special place in my heart. We had both been inmates in the Citadel Prison where we spent several months together during which I got to know him well. I came to realize that one could never free oneself of the bond of his affection. There was nothing sentimental or precious about Shuhdi; it was just that he was the kind of Communist you or any other Communist would have wished to be. I had never seen anyone as solid as he was. We often disagreed, but he was keen on drawing the line between our differences in stance and the fact of our being locked up together as prisoners of conscience.

Was this why Shuhdi enthralled me?

I didn't think this was the only reason. There was something special about Shuhdi, something I couldn't quite put into words. He always began by finding common grounds, then come what may, it wouldn't make any difference. So it was only natural that everyone should hold him in such esteem. As for his defense and the political case he made in prison on behalf of all the detainees, this meant he was exposing himself to the harshest punishment from the military tribunal that had been hastily formed to provide a cover-up for pre-determined penalization. He had run that risk in return for the political defense he made of his organization and of socialism, despite his support of Nasser's nationalist measures.

And there he was. The only thing separating us was the observation room in which my mere presence was a crime that I alone would pay the price for if found out by one of the monsters whom the grand reception had deranged, the effort they had exerted in the beatings making them pant audibly.

Shuhdi managed to turn over and pull himself together. I almost cried out, "Stay strong, Shuhdi. It's almost over, Shuhdi. Only a few minutes left." Then he raised himself on his elbows to avoid the madness of Officer Abd al-Latif Rushdi, who went on with his business, saying, "You still won't say you're a bitch, Shuhdi?"

You're only a few steps from the barber, then you'll have survived. If only you can put up with the few remaining blows. They'll crop off your hair, then dump you into the cell and your comrades will be able to save you until the cells are unlocked tomorrow.

When he finally managed to stand up, the soldiers ceased beating him. They let him take a few steps toward the barber at the inner gate of the prison. It was clear that they had started working on Shuhdi the minute he got out of the van, just as had happened to us when they inaugurated our first banquet of torture the minute we arrived at the prison, making us run an entire kilometer between two rows of soldiers beating us with sticks and belts.

Only it seemed that Shuhdi's bones had been totally broken. His giant body was struggling to get up, but just then Abd al-Latif Rushdi quickly served him a blow on the shoulder with his stick that made him lose his balance. Then he hit Shuhdi again, this time on the crown of his head, and he dropped to the ground.

All was confusion for a brief moment. Then Officer Murgan turned up with a paramedic. Murgan said, "Quick, a coramin shot. Quick, before he dies on us."

That could only mean one thing: Shuhdi had died. Behind the door, I could no longer stand and let my body crumple beneath me.

Ministry of Interior
Prison Authority
Abu Zaabal Prison Management
Re: Receipt of the corpse of a deceased prisoner
Date: June 16, 1960
To: Director of Forensic Medicine,
Zeinhom Morgue

Dear Sir,
Please find herewith the corpse of a prisoner under investigation, Shuhdi Attiya al-Shafie, may God have mercy on his soul, in response to the message sent to us by Abdin Police Station yesterday, as per your assignment for this purpose by the Deputy State Prosecutor.

Please duly sign receipt accordingly.

With utmost respect,
Sergeant George Aziz Basta
Chief Warden, Abu Zaabal Prison

Coming from Sergeant Hasan Mounir, there was nothing unusual in this brazenness, but that their impudence should reach the extent of moving Shuhdi's body to one of the cells and hanging above it a handwritten sign that read "Hospital" was altogether surreal. Sheer madness. But it had to be said that what Hasan Mounir was doing followed naturally on all that had happened before it. Had we not kept silent about the murder of Farid Haddad? Then again, what could we have done, given all that we were exposed to every day? What with the daily feasts of torture, we were all on the brink of death ourselves. They had succeeded in turning us into animals with no thought for anything other than staying on the right side of death, from which we were separated by only a minute or two.

At last, delegates from the public prosecutor's office arrived. I laughed when I heard the news. Why did they come and what were they going to do? Were they going to collaborate with the prison authorities in covering up the crime? The prosecutor's office hadn't taken the trouble when Farid Haddad was killed, nor had it bothered with us as we were being brutally tortured every day. Why then this compassion, finally, from his Excellency the Prosecutor?

I was the one who first saw Shuhdi after they had finished him. I was in Cell Three, to which we had been moved only a day before he was killed, when I heard the thud of a body crashing to the ground. I rushed to the peephole in the door. One soldier was telling another, "Lift him, lift him up with me."

"You lift him," came the answer.

Then another voice yelling, "Where's that son of a bitch, the paramedic?"

I could only see a small part of the courtyard by the main gate and was describing everything I saw to my colleagues in a whisper. I heard the voice of Amin the paramedic as he was thumping Shuhdi's giant outstretched body. Shuhdi was naked as the paramedic turned him over.

"Get up, boy. Be brave, now. Get up."

Then I heard that criminal Murgan shouting, "Quick, coramin, a coramin shot!"

"I gave it to him, sir. It's no use," the paramedic answered.

Would the prosecutor really investigate?

And would the prosecutor take down my testimony?

6

What was there between her and Abd al-Wahab? Try as Alia might to evade the question, it came back to haunt her. It had been easy for her keep up a regular correspondence with Abd al-Wahab over e-mail. But in person there was something about him she couldn't quite put her finger on that had stood between them from the minute she glimpsed him get up as she walked through the door of the coffee shop the night before.

She had talked herself into thinking he had come to Cairo to work on the project of the co-authored book collecting her aunt's papers and her father's journals and notes. Most of the time they had spent wandering through Gammaliya had been taken up by Abd al-Wahab's infatuation with the place, which made all the more sense when she read some pages of his book on Basra that he had given her the day before. The first pages that she read before falling asleep were mellow reminiscences about his childhood in the alleys of the old city, about the smell of its houses and its inhabitants' voices. In writing, he came across as warmer, perhaps even more tender. Yes, there was something that stood between them. Was it the age difference? "I doubt it," Alia reasoned. "He's a man, and a handsome one too. Can I be patient and keep a close watch on myself during his stay here in Cairo? I am free of him, whereas with Fouad al-Shafie it was the opposite, I couldn't imagine living without him. Even if I have a fling with him—a little crush never cracked anyone's bones!—he'll be leaving in ten days' time, and it'll all be over. But if I were to fall in love?"

He had called her at nine that morning to say he was going to go crazy if he didn't go right now to Gammaliya to rediscover it by daylight. He'd go alone, he added, and would call her when he got back. Before she could answer he had put down the receiver. She considered getting dressed and catching up with him there, to give him a surprise. But where would she find him?

Before parting with each other the previous night they had agreed that he should postpone his visit to the Egyptian Museum by a day. Instead, he would settle for spending two hours or so with her in the Mari Girgis neighborhood. This was all the time she could spare because she needed to make arrangements for her mother since she was going to be out most of the night at the gala on the Pyramid Plateau.

When she got home the night before, her mother was still asleep. Feeling her mother's bed and clothes and finding them dry, Alia reflected that her health had improved a lot. Her mother used to stay awake most of the night and Alia couldn't keep up with changing her underwear. But ever since she finished the chemotherapy treatment, she managed to sleep most of the night, from eight or nine in the evening until the following morning, and was steadily getting better. Alia was going to spend the whole day with her mother until her 9:30 p.m. rendezvous with Abd al-Wahab, when she'd join him for the gala at the Pyramids. She could get permission from the managing editor not to go to the office today. It wasn't going to be a problem: only the day before she'd submitted to him four articles, three of which were translated. The fourth article, which she herself had written about the New Year's Eve celebrations at the Pyramids based on the information she'd received from the press bureau, had already been published that day.

Her mother sensed her presence when she slipped into the room and tried to get up. Alia rushed to her and kissed her.

"Good morning, Mom! How are we doing today? Hope you woke up feeling nice and fresh." Watching her mother sit up, she smiled and said, "Just a second."

She went over to the radio and switched it on. Umm Kulthum's voice, suffused with coquettish joyfulness, flowed:

Take the hint from flowers—
How they speak volumes to lovers!

He was there to receive her the minute she alighted from the cab.

"I've really put you through a lot of trouble. I'll never forget all you've done for me since I landed in Cairo."

She let her hand rest in his for a minute. He wasn't in his coat but was wearing a navy blue woolen blazer, while she had come in the same leather jacket as the night before. She accepted his offer to have coffee before they set out for the gala.

As soon as they sat down she took out two tickets, which she pushed toward him with a smile.

"You'll be my guest tonight too. I just hope it won't be a fiasco."

"How could it, darling? It's an extravaganza presided over by the greatest gods of their day, in the embrace of the Sphinx and the Pyramids!"

"Oh, I worry about that man they brought from France, Jean-Michel Jarre, I just don't know what he'll get up to. I attended a press conference with him yesterday, before you arrived from Denmark. Instead of holding an Egyptian night, they brought in a foreigner."

Sipping his coffee, he broke in with, "What matters is that we'll be spending the evening together, and at your invitation. What do you say we have dinner before we set out?"

"We'll be late."

"I actually ordered before you got here. It's ready for us in the restaurant. Please come this way."

He got up and bowed theatrically. It was all she could do not to lean toward him and caress his tanned face, which looked alluring with its crown of chestnut hair gone silvery around the temples. This is what I haven't braced myself against, she thought inwardly—his gentleness, courtesy, sense of humor, and readiness to back off at the slightest hint from me.

The fried fish and rice, which came with lots of salads, were nice and hot.

"Did I pick the wrong dishes? I went over to the kitchen and found that this was the best they had."

"Oh, I enjoy fish. So, where did you go in the morning?"

"First, would you allow me to order wine to mark this historical night?"

"Feel free, Abd al-Wahab. But you keep saying all these difficult things."

"Difficult?"

"Yes, the historical stuff you go on about." She burst out laughing. He smiled out of courtesy, then it dawned on him what she meant and he laughed out just as she was about to apologize.

"Anyway," she continued, "this is some of the best fried bolti fish I've had, it reminds me of the fish you get in Alexandria. But let's finish quickly to catch up with *The Twelve Dreams of the Sun*."

"There you go saying historical things, too."

"Actually, it's the title of the show the Frenchman is putting on. He was brought over especially to choreograph and set the score for this 'historical show' as you would put it."

They finished their dinner, hurried out, and stopped the first cab. The driver asked for double the normal fare. Abd al-Wahab nodded then turned to her and murmured, "I still think you're the most beautiful surprise, Alia."

She smiled silently and nestled against his shoulder . Cairo sped before their eyes all aglitter in the chilly night. His tipsiness emboldened him and he leaned toward her.

"The most beautiful surprise, Alia, yes, the most beautiful."

You walked straight into that trap, she thought, as she shut her eyes. But the car ground to a halt just then and the driver turned to them with, "Can't go any further. You should just get on one of those vans taking people to the gala."

Abd al-Wahab gave her his arm to lean on as they wended their way, swaying slightly, to the armed forces van that was about to start moving and got in. Through the window he made out the indistinct outlines of the Great Pyramid, which came into sharper focus while the cars jostled around them on the tarmac. Everyone got off the van and went up what seemed to be wooden stairs, finally arriving in a wide plaza littered with large tents and teeming with hundreds of tourists, soldiers, and young men and women. Abd al-Wahab was startled to see the Great

Pyramid right in front of him, as he stood amid dozens of other people. Despite the freezing weather the women were bare-armed and -throated in their heavily bejeweled evening dresses, and all sorts of perfumes wafted from them.

"The show's started," Alia announced. "Shall we watch from here or go in and catch our breath?"

"So that's what these tents are for, to have a little rest in? Strange."

The loud music mixed with the cacophony made by the people leaving the tents and the others standing around in the plaza. Alia led the way, pulling him behind her by the hand. Laser beams were projected all over the mass of the Great Pyramid while the stage was set in the center of the open space to allow for viewing from any vantage point. A young man with a scarf around his neck was on stage, bouncing and clowning around while playing the organ, the strains of which echoed into the vast desert.

In front of them were three wide screens, each showing a different view of the stones of the Pyramids. The musician, flooded in light, swayed right and left as he moved between the organ and the accordion, even nudging the huge drummer off his chair with a smile to beat at the instrument for a few seconds, apparently in a show of virtuosity. The screen closest to them bore the gigantic face of a cat, no doubt intended to represent an ancient Egyptian god. The electronic music piercing the desert air sent ripples among the crowds of young people who greeted it with cheers. Projected on the second screen was a semblance of an Egyptian peasant woman in kitschy colors, while the third screen showed what looked like a minaret.

"I'm really sorry. They've turned the Pyramid Plateau into a discotheque," Alia murmured as she leaned toward him.

"You're right—the biggest discotheque in the world. It's so tacky!"

Alia linked her arm with his and pressed it apologetically. She led him to the tent set up by the Ministry of Culture for its guests. Each of the official institutions had its own tent, and the interior of the Ministry of Culture one resembled a hotel ballroom or cafeteria. Dozens of guests in evening dress sat around the tables sipping tea and coffee and chattering raucously. Alia chose the nearest table.

"Again, I'm very sorry for this fiasco. It's such a scandal," she reiterated, leaning toward him.

"Yes, it's utterly tacky. But we mustn't let it spoil our evening together."

"Our 'historical' evening, Abd al-Wahab!"

When they had soaked up some warmth they took off their jackets then ordered tea to follow the coffee they had already had. It was then that she felt dizzy. It was not sleepiness but a mellow drowsiness she got whenever she felt snug. She looked at her watch with some effort, and Abd al-Wahab did too just then. It was close to midnight, so they joined the others pouring out of the tent. All the lights were switched off and the music had stopped. When he drew her to him she didn't resist and even leaned her head against his shoulder and shut her eyes. When Abd al-Wahab kissed her on the cheek, she returned his kiss. But the crazy young man who was conducting the band spoiled it all soon enough, electrifying the atmosphere with his music and clowning to the accompaniment of the laser show. The next tune was a pop dance one and the young crowd bounced around to it. Even Alia couldn't help joining in for a few minutes before accompanying Abd al-Wahab back to the tent.

They ordered coffee and took off their jackets.

"I read about fifty pages of your book on Basra last night," she said, "and found it very well written. It's actually more eloquent than speech, your speech, I mean."

Realizing that she had blundered into a bit of nonsense, she giggled nervously. He smiled quizzically. "Should I take this as praise or criticism?"

"As praise, of course. Though I was very tired, as you know, I couldn't put down the book."

"I still insist that, for me at least, it's a historical evening, Alia."

They laughed together over their running joke, then Alia stopped to say, "In principle, I consent to the idea of a book combining my father's diaries and my aunt's papers. So now we just need to get on with selecting and editing."

"Great, darling. Before I leave, you will have the manuscript of the book in your hands. I'd be grateful if you'd agree to meet with me on a daily basis while I'm in town. I'm sure we can get the work done because the two of us have read these documents many times over. I suggest you write the introduction and give an account of the journey of your father's papers. Then we can get to the selection process."

"What do you say we start immediately?" she broke in.

"I've actually started and we'll go over my selections together," he said with a smile as he drew his face closer to her across the table.

Her smile widened as she surrendered to his handgrip before they got up. "I apologize again for what that foreigner did. Actually, I feel like going home. Do you mind?"

He helped her with her jacket, then they slipped out. Outdoors the hubbub was escalating, what with the music, the laser show, the fireworks, huge screens, the crowds of young people dancing, and others standing around cheering.

When they had finally got out and were on their way westward to the slope that led to the Sphinx, a fog suddenly descended and thickened to envelop the audience, the band, and indeed the Great Pyramid itself. Only the electronic music rose above the fog, and the fog in turn gave the din a greater intensity. It was as if the band was playing for the desert, the audience having been startled into silence by the fog. Alia held onto Abd al-Wahab's arm firmly as they threaded their way gingerly, barely making out what lay immediately ahead of them. Is this the curse of the pharaohs? Alia wondered. They proceeded slowly among others who were just as bewildered, until they wound up on an asphalt slope. They got past the Great Pyramid and continued toward the Sphinx. As they approached and its outlines grew more distinct, Alia could not believe what she was seeing. At first, she put it down to the fog, but her impression hardened into certainty when they came in full view of the Sphinx.

She snatched her hand away from Abd al-Wahab's arm and cried, "Where's the Sphinx's head? Am I dreaming? Isn't this the Sphinx—decapitated?"

"Yes, it *is* the Sphinx, and its head is gone!"

He followed her across the low stone wall and came up beside her as she stood staring at the Sphinx's two forelegs, on which it crouched without a head, the rest of its body being otherwise intact. They've decapitated it without a single drop of blood, Alia reflected. Can it really be true that they beheaded it bloodlessly, and on this very night, while we were celebrating *The Twelve Dreams of the Sun*? Oh, what's been happening to me ever since I met you, Abd al-Wahab?

"Isn't this the Sphinx without its head, Abd al-Wahab? Answer me! I can't believe it," she cried out.

"Yes, darling, it is indeed the Sphinx without a head."

"This is the second head since you got here, Abd al-Wahab."

"You mean after your father's head, which he lost on the borders? Actually, it's the third, if we count the head of Umm al-Ghulam's son."

She was overcome by vertigo and sank to her knees before the Sphinx, while the fog gradually cleared to give way to the garish laser beams piercing the screens erected against the Great Pyramid.

By Way
of Epilogue

ANOTHER MORNING—THOUGH NOT *like any other morning.*

I open my eyes before the sun rises, in those few moments when I feel the refreshing chill in the air.

At first, I cannot believe it when the two small, soft palms touch my head and start tenderly pulling the skin off the top of the iron bridge it is stuck to. I do not even scream but give a series of short gasps until my head has been actually set free. I shut my eyes as I confront what I had thought was an impossibility ever since I barely made it onto the last carriage of the train and blissfully climbed up between two carriages and from there up onto the roof, where I joined my companions who were sitting around eating and smoking.

To this minute I still remember everything that went on between us. I remember recounting that I'd caught the last carriage of the last train— "You may've seen me racing toward the train, relying on myself alone." It's time I got some rest after all, I threw in, because this might be my last trip.

I remember, too, how I sat there overjoyed, wondering just how to celebrate. I got up and broke into a sprightly dance, bounding down the roof of the train, with my eyes shut for a few seconds and my arms outstretched to bask in the mild daylight, the sky above open and clear. Then I'd shut my eyes again and reopen them before leaping across the gap between one carriage and another. But one time, when I opened my eyes, I did not manage to duck at the right moment, so the first iron bridge hacked off my head. At first, I sensed my body separating from me, and how it pained me that it kept staggering on its own with no control over its steps until I fell under the wheels, while my head was impaled atop the iron bridge with my eyes open, gazing toward the south.

And here I am, having surrendered myself to the two small palms that lift me up as I try to open my eyes and resist the vertigo that's overcome me. When I come in contact with her chest, I sense the roundness of her breasts as the sharp fragrance of her body suffuses me.

Is it time I went to sleep, finally?

My head bounces, at first slowly, then faster. As I start gasping again and try to open my eyes, I catch a whiff of the bloody smell of the skin of my head. I mumble as the pain rises treacherously, but she draws me tighter to her chest. It seems to me that it is her arms that are now enfolding me, embracing my head to her sheltering chest.

From the quiver of her hair across my forehead I can tell she's going down the stairs of the iron bridge, now that she's set me free, then crossing the station, almost flying, with my head. The sound of many footsteps in the distance reaches me and I try to disentangle myself from her arms to get a glimpse of whoever is chasing us, but she draws me even tighter into her embrace and I surrender to the softness of her chest as her exhalations wash over me.

Thrusting my head between her breasts, I muse that she's probably one of the schoolgirls who used to stand in groups staring at me impaled on the iron bridge while they waited for the train that took them to their schools. Several times it seemed to me that one of them in particular—a girl whose heavy black hair was pulled back into a thick braid that dangled down to her waist—repeatedly stood gazing at me. In fact, I remember that she often drew up on her own down the platform with her amber eyes saying all there was to say as she fastened them on me. As for me, my eyes would soon part with hers when the sun rose and I received my first feast of torture.

Could this be her, the one who often drew up to me with her thick braid dangling down to her waist?

In any case, here I am, apparently set free, even if there are others chasing us. I listen out for their fragmented shouts and receding clamor while the girl carrying me dashes faster and faster until she's past the railway crossing. Then she runs for dear life.

Sahil Rawd al-Farag–Sixth of October City
October 1998–September 2001

Translator's Afterword

A mong the longstanding, albeit repeatedly contested, pro-
tocols of Egyptian literary life is the labeling of writers by
generation. Introducing *al-Qissa al-qasira fi-l-sab'iniyat*
('The Short Story in the 1970s'), a 1982 anthology he edited that
was to be seminal in launching the 1970s generation of writers,
novelist and critic Edwar al-Kharrat (b. 1926) insightfully suggests
that the generational criterion may not be germane to the "new sen-
sibility" he locates in these writers' work, which can be traced back
to much earlier texts, even in the absence of a direct line of descent.
But he rightly observes that the social and political climate within
which the consciousness of these writers—in their early twenties
in the 1970s—was formed is crucial for understanding, if not
accounting for, their literary production. Given that Mahmoud Al-
Wardani (b. 1950) is a member of this generation—one of his short
stories was in fact included in the anthology—some background
about the period, not least since it has a bearing on *Heads Ripe for
Plucking*, should be provided here.

For the 1970s generation, the pivotal event was the 1967 War and the signal moment was the student movement that arose, in large measure as a response, on the campuses of several state universities. The activism on the campuses reached a crescendo in January 1972 when President Sadat made a speech in which he blamed deferring action to liberate Egyptian territories occupied by Israel in 1967 on the Indo-Pakistani War and the consequent "fog" that clouded the political scene. Sit-ins that continued for several days were held mainly at Cairo and Ain Shams universities, and when these were forcefully dispersed and a number of students arrested, an all-night student sit-in was held in Tahrir Square in downtown Cairo, which was also broken up the following day. The January 1972 uprising—in which Al-Wardani participated—drove home the need for decisive action to free the occupied territories, as Ahmed Abdalla, one of the uprising's leaders, observed in his *The Student Movement and National Politics in Egypt 1923–1973*. Student activism was to continue in various forms after the 1973 War, spurred by Sadat's political and economic rapprochement with the west and the peace accords with Israel. It was these transformations in the country, as much as the transformations in the activists themselves—some of whom were later to embrace the very agendas they had set out to contest—that led Arwa Salih, one of the prominent figures in the movement who committed suicide in 1997, to designate the 1970s generation *al-Mubtasarun* ('The Premature Ones'), which is the title of her 1996 book of reflections on that period.

Al-Wardani's experience serving in the 1973 War arranging for the burial of dead soldiers is at the core of the title section of his collection of short stories, *al-Sayr fi-l-hadiqa laylan* ('To Walk in the Garden by Night,' 1984), and was later to be developed in *Nawbat ruju'* ('Call to Quarters,' 1990), his first novel which also explores the impact of the student movement on the 1970s generation. By his second novel, *Ra'ihat al-burtuqal* ('Scent of Oranges,' 1992), the sense of being haunted by the unburied, here a child in the protagonist's arms, and of political harassment for an oppositional past would become elements in a quasi-surrealist tableau of disorientation and menace. The 1970s student movement was to resurface in his 1998 novel *al-Rawd al-'atir* ('The Perfumed Garden'), to which one of the stories in *Heads Ripe for Plucking* is a sequel.

The Arabic title of *Heads Ripe for Plucking*, *Awan al-qitaf*, which denotes 'season for plucking,' alludes to the infamous, oft-quoted sermon—"I see heads before me that are ripe and ready for plucking"—with which al-Hajjaj al-Thaqafi, one of the governors of Iraq under the Umayyad Caliphate, addressed the Kufans before quelling a mutiny. The impaled head—presumably of a worker or even day laborer—in the frame story of the novel empathically bears witness to various forms of oppression in six stories that unfold over the three sections of the novel. Although as part and parcel of the novel's experimentation the stories are not arranged in historical sequence, they chart a wide chronological spectrum that can only be briefly noted here. The first story, the earliest chronologically, centers on what is arguably the primary beheading in Arabo-Islamic history, that of al-Husayn, Prophet Muhammad's grandson. A stage in the formation of the schism between Sunni and Shi'ite Islam that traces back to his father Ali, the conflict that led to al-Husayn's murder was both a political and a spiritual one pivoted on the criterion for succession to the caliphate after the death of the Prophet. The fourth story lies at the other end of the chronological spectrum in that it takes us into a futuristic dystopia where citizens are disciplined through a procedure that literalizes the metaphor of brainwashing.

The four remaining stories cover between them the second half of the twentieth century in Egypt. In the second story, the decapitation of the man who returns from Saudi Arabia by his wife and her lover highlights the far-reaching effect of migrant labor to oil-rich Arab countries on Egyptian society since the 1970s, specifically the dissolution and alienation in the family sphere resulting from the work stint in the Gulf. The third story unfolds under the shadow of the sea change in Egypt during the Sadat years, in particular the regime's Open Door policy of liberalizing the economy after the socialist orientation of the Nasser years. The bread riots of January 18 and 19, 1977—that Sadat preferred to refer to as the "intifada of thieves"—in which the schoolboy in this story gets caught were triggered by the government's decision, under pressure from the IMF, to cut subsidies on basic commodities and foodstuffs. The grievances of the demonstrators were distilled in scathing slogans that, as cited in the fourth story, did not spare the ostentation of Sadat and his wife Gihan, the self-styled First Lady.

The fifth story takes us back to the years following the Free Officers' July 1952 Revolution and the large-scale imprisonment of Communists and left-wing intellectuals and activists in 1959, the detainees being released in stages in the mid-1960s. Based on documentary sources, this story recapitulates the vicissitudes of the relationship between the various Communist organizations and the new regime whose authoritarian nature manifested itself in a series of repressive measures culminating in the 1959 arrests. At the center of this story is the death under torture of Shuhdi Attiya al-Shafie, one of the charismatic leaders of the Communist movement, but the text also refers to other historical figures such as the poet Fouad Haddad, the intellectual Louis Awad, and the medical doctor Farid Haddad. A spin-off from the fifth story in *Heads Ripe for Plucking* was

Al-Wardani's following book, a non-fiction account of the Democratic Movement for National Liberation entitled *Hatitu* (2007), this being the acronym of the Arabic name of that Communist organization, al-Haraka al-Dimuqratiyya li-l-Taharrur al-Watani.

The sixth story in the novel harks back to the 1970s—a decade already highlighted in the third story—by 're-membering' the activist aunt Iqbal who committed suicide, quotations from whose writings are drawn, as the novelist acknowledges, from *Saratan al-rawh* ('Cancer of the Soul,' 1998), the posthumously published book by Arwa Salih. As previously noted, this story takes up where Al-Wardani's *al-Rawd al-'atir* left off. That earlier novel had as its protagonist Iqbal Bakri, an activist from the 1970s generation who, after a period of self-imposed exile in Germany, returns to Cairo where she lives in the family apartment with Shaker, her divorced brother then struggling with an unfinished scenario about the nationalist leader Ahmad Urabi before he moves to Kuwait on the eve of the 1991 Gulf War. On a more contemporary note, the two severed heads here, Shaker's and the Sphinx's, emblematize, in the former case, American neocolonialism in the region as witnessed in the 1991 Gulf War and, in the latter, globalization's spreading of kitschy art and representations of heritage that stand in stark contrast to the tour of Islamic Cairo that Alia and Abd al-Wahab take earlier in the story—themes Al-Wardani was to revisit in a different vein in his next novel, *Musiqa al-mul* ('Mall Music,' 2005).

The polyphony of voices in the novel and the different styles it comprises, for which it was critically lauded, pose one of the major challenges to its translator. Certain *sui generis* issues come with the territory of translating an Arabic text that exploits the classical/colloquial diglossia of the language, but what was at stake here went beyond that. The novel brings a spectrum of registers, whether in classical Arabic—from the diction and stylistic features of medieval chronicles in the story about al-Husayn to the contemporary, pedestrian language of the man who returns from Saudi Arabia—or in the varieties of colloquial Arabic usage in some of the dialogues, not least the teenager's, and in the coded jargon associated with a given context, such as prison torture or drug dens. How the different stories relate to each other and to the central theme of the novel is a matter of interpretation, but my task was to retain the contrast of tenor and linguistic texture. To that end, I translated longitudinally, as it were, working on a story across the three sections of the novel before moving to the next one, in order to sustain the register and tone of each. If a high register comprising archaisms seemed apropos for the narrative about al-Husayn's martyrdom, a dilemma remained regarding the extent to which I would render the text fluent when it came to translating the rest of the novel with its variously modern and contemporary settings.

It was not so much a question of differentiating the textures of the five remaining stories from each other, but whether, in so doing, I would also emphasize their 'translatedness.' My attention to this issue was compelled by Lawrence Venuti's argument in *The Translator's Invisibility* as well as *The Scandals of Translation* for a "foreignizing" translation strategy that would resist the "domesticating," fluent approach favored in the Anglo-American literary arena whereby the status of a text as translated is occluded, hence reinforcing the cultural, political, and economic hegemony of Anglophone nations. While agreeing with Venuti's position in its broad outlines, my sense is that when it comes to translating Arabic literature into English, specifically, the strategy he recommends should be used sparingly rather than consistently. The perceived exceptionalism of the Arab world in English-speaking nations—its portrayal as the "barbarian ramming the gates of" civilization, as Michael Toler put it in critique of Venuti's position—in any case works against the assimilation of the text.* The array of Arab historical and cultural references that *Heads Ripe for Plucking* brings also registers its difference, further highlighted here by the inclusion of a translator's afterword and a glossary. But as far as the translation itself is concerned, I adapted the foreignizing strategy and applied it selectively. On the one hand, I avoided placing excessive ethnographic markers—for example, I transliterated the word 'sabil' and inserted an explanatory gloss into the text after it rather than according it an entry in the glossary—and, on the other, I occasionally intimated a defamiliarizing Arabic turn of phrase here, and indicated the trace of a proverb there, within a translation that largely sought parallel idioms and registers in English for each story and narrative voice.

Written for an Arabic-language readership and completed in September 2001, *Awan al-qitaf* is an oppositional text that pits itself primarily against oppression in the Arab world. The Anglophone reader of *Heads Ripe for Plucking* receives the novel in the post-9/11 world. Several times while working on the translation, I worried that aspects of the text might be read against the grain in the current western climate of suspicion surrounding the Middle East, serving to confirm ready stereotypes of violence. Would the narrative about al-Husayn involving the schism between Shi'ites and Sunnis and the refractions of the 1991 Gulf War in the sixth story automatically activate stereotypes that have gained further currency since the 2003 Iraq War? But then I reasoned that this would be a reductive reading of the novel, and not solely on account of the text's offering a representation of that earlier western military incursion in Iraq from the vantage point of its victims. It would be a skewed reading that overlooks the instances of torture and oppression drawn from the contexts of America, Europe, and Asia mulled over by the impaled head at the beginning of Part Three in a catalog that, if written now, would likely have included Abu Ghraib and Guantánamo. Ultimately, the note of qualified hope on which the text closes, "by way of epilogue," elicits a commitment to emancipatory humanism. And therein lies the novel's timeliness.

I am grateful to the editors at AUC Press—Neil Hewison, Nadia Naqib, and Noha Mohammed—for the efficiency with which they handled the manuscript. I am indebted to Peter Daniel for many suggestions generously offered. I checked the transliteration of certain names in the story about al-Husayn against *The Caliphate of Yazīd b. Mu'āwiyah*, I. K. A. Howard's translation of the relevant volume of al-Tabarī's *Tarikh al-rusul wa-l-muluk*, although the transliteration system followed here is different. The moral support I received from Fatma Moussa-Mahmoud, the late professor of English literature and literary translator, who nominated my previous translated book for a State Incentive Award, was invaluable in motivating the present work.

*See Michael Toler, "The Ethics of Cultural Representation: The Maghribi Novel in Translation," *The Journal of North African Studies* 6, no. 3 (2001): 48-69; quotation p. 66.

Glossary

Awad, Louis (1914–1990): Literary critic, poet, novelist, and public intellectual, he was dismissed from his post as professor of English literature at Cairo University in the 1954 purge of academics suspected of leftist affiliations, and imprisoned in 1959 until the mid-1960s.

Bandung: The Asian-African Conference held at Bandung, Indonesia, in 1955 promoted cultural and economic cooperation between the decolonized countries of these two continents, respect for human rights and the sovereignty of nations, and world peace.

Free Officers: The group of army officers, including Gamal Abd al-Nasser, later president of Egypt, who led the 1952 Revolution and were to occupy key positions in the new regime.

Haddad, Fouad (1927–1985): One of the foremost 20th-century poets writing in colloquial Egyptian Arabic who published some thirty collections of poetry informed by commitment to socialist themes, he was imprisoned in the early 1950s, then again from 1959 to 1964.

Kafr al-Dawwar: This Delta town witnessed strikes by workers from a textile factory demanding better work conditions in August 1952, culminating in the Free Officers' executing two of the strikers and imprisoning several others.

Qarmatian state: A dissident group that broke away from the Shi'ite Ismaili movement at the end of the ninth century, the Qarmatians founded a state in Bahrain that lasted for about two centuries.

Sawad: An old name in Arabic for Iraq, the word was also used to denote the cultivated area in a given region. In the novel it refers to Iraq.

Urabi, Ahmad (1840?–1911): Army officer and leader of the 1882 nationalist uprising against European influence in Egypt that demanded greater Egyptian representation in the Turco-Circassian dominated army and constitutionalism. The movement was defeated by the British, who occupied Egypt that same year.

Modern Arabic Literature
from the American University in Cairo Press

Ibrahim Abdel Meguid *Birds of Amber* • *Distant Train*
No One Sleeps in Alexandria • *The Other Place*
Yahya Taher Abdullah *The Collar and the Bracelet* • *The Mountain of Green Tea*
Leila Abouzeid *The Last Chapter*
Hamdi Abu Golayyel *Thieves in Retirement*
Yusuf Abu Rayya *Wedding Night*
Ahmed Alaidy *Being Abbas el Abd*
Idris Ali *Dongola* • *Poor*
Radwa Ashour *Granada*
Ibrahim Aslan *The Heron* • *Nile Sparrows*
Alaa Al Aswany *Chicago* • *The Yacoubian Building*
Fadhil al-Azzawi *Cell Block Five* • *The Last of the Angels*
Liana Badr *The Eye of the Mirror*
Hala El Badry *A Certain Woman* • *Muntaha*
Salwa Bakr *The Golden Chariot* • *The Man from Bashmour* • *The Wiles of Men*
Halim Barakat *The Crane*
Hoda Barakat *Disciples of Passion* • *The Tiller of Waters*
Mourid Barghouti *I Saw Ramallah*
Mohamed El-Bisatie *Clamor of the Lake* • *Houses Behind the Trees* • *Hunger*
A Last Glass of Tea • *Over the Bridge*
Mansoura Ez Eldin *Maryam's Maze*
Ibrahim Farghali *The Smiles of the Saints*
Hamdy el-Gazzar *Black Magic*
Tawfiq al-Hakim *The Essential Tawfiq al-Hakim*
Abdelilah Hamdouchi *The Final Bet*
Fathy Ghanem *The Man Who Lost His Shadow*
Randa Ghazy *Dreaming of Palestine*
Gamal al-Ghitani *Pyramid Texts* • *The Zafarani Files* • *Zayni Barakat*
Yahya Hakki *The Lamp of Umm Hashim*
Bensalem Himmich *The Polymath* • *The Theocrat*
Taha Hussein *The Days* • *A Man of Letters* • *The Sufferers*
Sonallah Ibrahim *Cairo: From Edge to Edge* • *The Committee* • *Zaat*
Yusuf Idris *City of Love and Ashes*
Denys Johnson-Davies *The AUC Press Book of Modern Arabic Literature*
In a Fertile Desert: Modern Writing from the United Arab Emirates
Under the Naked Sky: Short Stories from the Arab World
Said al-Kafrawi *The Hill of Gypsies*

Sahar Khalifeh *The End of Spring*
The Image, the Icon, and the Covenant • *The Inheritance*
Edwar al-Kharrat *Rama and the Dragon* • *Stones of Bobello*
Betool Khedairi *Absent*
Mohammed Khudayyir *Basrayatha*
Ibrahim al-Koni *Anubis* • *Gold Dust* • *The Seven Veils of Seth*
Naguib Mahfouz *Adrift on the Nile* • *Akhenaten: Dweller in Truth*
Arabian Nights and Days • *Autumn Quail* • *The Beggar*
The Beginning and the End • *Cairo Modern*
The Cairo Trilogy: Palace Walk, Palace of Desire, Sugar Street
Children of the Alley • *The Day the Leader Was Killed*
The Dreams • *Dreams of Departure* • *Echoes of an Autobiography*
The Harafish • *The Journey of Ibn Fattouma* • *Karnak Café*
Khan al-Khalili • *Khufu's Wisdom* • *Life's Wisdom* • *Midaq Alley* • *Miramar*
Mirrors • *Morning and Evening Talk* • *Naguib Mahfouz at Sidi Gaber*
Respected Sir • *Rhadopis of Nubia* • *The Search*
The Seventh Heaven • *Thebes at War* • *The Thief and the Dogs*
The Time and the Place • *Voices from the Other World* • *Wedding Song*
Mohamed Makhzangi *Memories of a Meltdown*
Alia Mamdouh *The Loved Ones* • *Naphtalene*
Selim Matar *The Woman of the Flask*
Ibrahim al-Mazini *Ten Again*
Yousef Al-Mohaimeed *Wolves of the Crescent Moon*
Ahlam Mosteghanemi *Chaos of the Senses* • *Memory in the Flesh*
Mohamed Mustagab *Tales from Dayrut*
Buthaina Al Nasiri *Final Night*
Ibrahim Nasrallah *Inside the Night*
Haggag Hassan Oddoul *Nights of Musk*
Mohamed Mansi Qandil *Moon over Samarqand*
Abd al-Hakim Qasim *Rites of Assent*
Somaya Ramadan *Leaves of Narcissus*
Lenin El-Ramly *In Plain Arabic*
Ghada Samman *The Night of the First Billion*
Rafik Schami *Damascus Nights*
Khairy Shalaby *The Lodging House*
Miral al-Tahawy *Blue Aubergine* • *Gazelle Tracks* • *The Tent*
Bahaa Taher *As Doha Said* • *Love in Exile*
Fuad al-Takarli *The Long Way Back*
M.M. Tawfik *Murder in the Tower of Happiness*
Mahmoud Al-Wardani *Heads Ripe for Plucking*
Latifa al-Zayyat *The Open Door*